A GUN ROARED

Blackie held the smoking gun in his right hand as the poker dealer slumped to the floor.

Bedlam broke loose. Men yelled and dived for cover. Others stood frozen, too startled to move. Blackie stood astride the dead dealer's body, still gripping the pistol in his right hand, as the two deputy marshals plowed through the crowd. His other gun was out now, and his black eyes were blazing.

"Hand over those guns, cowpunch," ordered one of the marshals. "You can't get away with that here. This is Abilene."

"This is Texas, mister," Blackie said. "I can get away with anything I want!"

LONG RIDE TO ABILENE

●

William Hopson

MB

A MACFADDEN-BARTELL BOOK

THIS BOOK IS THE COMPLETE TEXT
OF THE ORIGINAL EDITION

MACFADDEN BOOKS are published by
Macfadden-Bartell Corporation
A subsidiary of Bartell Media Corporation
205 East 42nd Street, New York, New York, 10017

CHAPTER ONE

THE FIELD covered twelve acres of what once had been flat prairie land, and it was that time of year when the crops had been laid by. But Jude's father firmly believed that no son ever should be idle for a moment, particularly on a dry land farm; a big, brutal, hulking man who was a hell-roaring drunken devil one moment and a God-fearing, Bible-quoting fanatic the next. That was why Jude still worked in the field that afternoon when the Texas trail herd lu...

His father was a good farmer; ...
to the fences to squeeze int...

to come abreast of where he stood. He saw two men riding at the head—point—and the thought unconsciously pushed itself into his mind that they were leaders, like the lead steers that plodded a few yards behind. The dust began there, gathered in intensity and roiled back over and alongside the long lumbering line of cattle; so thick that the men back along the flanks wore their bandanas up over their noses. He had seen them close up once, and they looked like desperados.

A rider back along the herd suddenly spurred out of the dust and came toward him at a lope. Jude stood there watching him, the tingle again hitting his spine. It was the first time one of them ever had come this close. He knew that they hated farmers—whom they contemptuously referred to as "damned sod-busting nesters"—and the farmers hated them equally as much. One hundred fifty miles to the north lay Abilene, in the big flush of its cattle and railroad boom; where the last of the starving buffalo the ignominious job of hauling the once had slaughtered by

so instead of planting close
...into the field every possible stalk, he
planted wide, leaving a twelve-foot belt between the fences
and the green. And Jude had been plowing this belt, pushing
back the weeds by turning them under, making long bright
furrows in the cool earth.

Jude said, "Whoa, boys," and eased the span of big bays
to a halt. They were sleek, well fed, and as strong as oxen.
That was one thing about his father: His was the best farm
and had the best equipment in the country. But then, Jude
thought, he'd got the jump on so many of the hundreds of
others who were wrestling life and some kind of future se-
curity from the soil. Jude's mother had furnished the money.
And a fanatical devotion to hard work.

Jude wrapped the lines around the handle and walked
over to the fence, placing a dirt-encrusted shoe on the lower
strand. He leaned there, his eyes on the herd. This was the
third one there had passed within two weeks and each time
a strange tingling went up along his young spine at the sight.
There was something about those wild, longhorn cattle, and
the ragged riders, as wild-looking as the steers, that stirred
the imagination. They were free men who owed the world
nothing.

Jude leaned over the top strand and drank in the sight.

A half-mile to the east of him the leaders were beginning

a hell-roaring town ... hunters, now reduced to the whitened bones of the animals they ... the thousands, mingled with tough, drunken trail drivers up from the south from long drives and tearing the town apart in wild sprees.

The cowmen hated the flatland farmers for plowing under the range, and the farmers hated them because, when they came through, sometimes pure hatred sent a herd trampling down fences and fields and sucking up the few head of stock the farmers owned. They had protested, cursed, and threatened helplessly—all in the face of contemptuous grins as the herd, taking their stock with it, moved on. They were helpless to do anything about it, and that helplessness alone fired their hatred to pitch heat and caused them to steal and butcher.

The rider came on, pulling his sweaty claybank to a halt beside the fence, and Jude thought he had never seen such a magnificently wild figure of a man. He was tall in the saddle, about twenty-eight, and had the blackest hair a man ever saw . . . though just now it was so shaggy it almost covered his ears. His faded flannel shirt was out at the elbows, and over the left breast was a large tear, exposing a six-inch area of browned skin covered with a mat of black hair. His leather chaps were held together only by a patchwork of rawhide thongs, and one spur on a worn boot had lost a rowel. It had been replaced with a fifty-cent piece of silver. The man wore two guns.

"Hello, nester," he said.

"Howdy," Jude said.

"Seen any herds passing by lately?"

"Three."

"When?"

Jude took out a nearly full tobacco sack and rolled himself a smoke. He caught the almost hungry, quickening look in the man's black eyes, a brief, hidden flicker the rider of the claybank hadn't intended him to see. Jude held out the sack, dangling on the end of a string. "Smoke?"

"Thanks." The rider lifted reins and touched a rowel to the off side of the horse. It sidled over and the man bent from the saddle, straightening again. He rolled, took the proffered match, sighed and held out the sack.

"You can keep it," Jude said. "I got plenty more."

The rider reached into a pocket and brought out a silver dollar. He flipped it through the air.

"I said you could keep it," Jude said.

"Won't take cowman money, eh?" asked the other. A faint touch of amusement had come into his eyes.

"I said I got plenty more."

"I see," replied the other, and for the first time he smiled. It was an easy-going, friendly grin. "Thanks, nester. About those cattle. When?"

Jude shifted his weight to the other foot and put another elbow over the top strand. "First about three weeks ago. Two miles east of here. Busted down all the fences and stole all the stock. Second about a week ago. The third day before yesterday. Same track you're following."

"See the brand on that last herd?" His voice had become sharp.

"Two of their steers strayed over this way. NP on the left hip. No road brand."

"Hmm." A pause while the rider smoked thoughtfully. He turned in the saddle. One of the men riding at point had broken away too and was loping toward them. The two-gunman turned his attention to Jude again. "What happened to the two strays?" he asked.

"One hind quarter is over in our meat house," Jude said calmly. "The others are scattered around."

The rider leaned back and laughed. It was a rich laugh,

and somehow Jude liked him, even if he was one of the men who were sworn enemies of the farmers. "You damned nesters," he chuckled. "Good Texas beef must taste good after salt pork."

Jude felt himself begin to freeze up a little. "We eat a lot of chickens and kill a pig now and then and got a garden."

The rider looked down, amused tolerance in his eyes. "Okay, nester. I'm hunkered. How far is it to Abilene?"

Jude lifted a left elbow and pointed, a course of about twenty degrees east from the one followed by the herd. "Hundred and fifty miles. You'll come in about ten-fifteen miles to the west the way you're traveling."

"Thanks."

The rider turned in the saddle as the second man came galloping up. One look at him told Jude that this man was the boss. He was tall, about six feet two, ragged as the others were ragged, with a long drooping mustache and a pair of piercing blue eyes. Authority showed in every movement of his body.

"Well, Blackie?" he snapped. "What'd the kid say?"

"Day before yesterday."

This would refer to the NP herd. "Late, almost dark," Jude added. "They camped four miles ahead at Gramma Creek."

"So they got in ahead of us?" the tall man said.

The other nodded. "I reckon. And if one of them gets drunk in town and talks loose, such as admitting they stampeded us, I'm going to have a little score to settle with Harrison."

"How far to Abilene and where?" rapped out the foreman.

"Kid says hundred and fifty miles and swing 'em a bit to the east."

The piercing blue eyes stared down at the overalled figure still leaning over the top strand. "How the hell do you know?" he demanded.

"I reckon I've been there," Jude said calmly.

The two-gun rider broke into a soft laugh, and then finished, grinning: "Hunkered you, Shelby! He sure hunkered you that time."

The trail boss saw no humor in the situation. He stared coldly at Jude again, then abruptly wheeled his horse and gigged in the spurs. Something in his manner indicated that he expected the other rider to follow, but the black-haired man called Blackie didn't. Something in *his* manner said that here was an hombre who kow-towed to no man.

"That's Nute Shelby. Trail boss," he said. He had lifted a leg and had been sitting with it curled around the saddle horn. Now he lowered it, and found the stirrup with a worn boot toe, preparatory to taking leave. He looked down again, past Jude's shoulder to where the silver dollar stood on its edge, half buried in the dirt.

"Pick up the dollar, kid," he said.

"You pick it up," Jude replied. "I told you I got plenty."

The rider laughed, and at that moment there came a new sound in the rustle of the corn back of Jude. His father had sneaked up on him again.

CHAPTER TWO

THE ELDER Gordon was in his mid-fifties and a powerfully built man. He had the solid bone of the soil worker with big gnarled hands, and in one of those hands he carried a twenty-foot length of coiled blacksnake whip of shiny plaited leather with an eighteen-inch hickory stock. He was dark, though not quite so dark as the rider of the claybank, covered now with a short stubble of pepper-shot whiskers. Jude's mother had been auburn-haired and freckled, and it was from her that he had inherited his own reddish hair and the mass of freckles. In moments of drunken frenzy John Gordon had many times roared at her that the damned brat couldn't have been his because it didn't look like him.

It was easy to see that the older man had been drinking heavily. Jude knew he had been running off a batch of stuff in the barn still that afternoon, which also accounted for the prosperity of the Gordon farm. John Gordon's neighbors for miles around beat a path to his door to buy the corn whiskey that came from the still. Gordon was jokingly known as the "corn farmer," and not without good reason. It accounted for that twelve acres now lazing greenly in the afternoon sun.

"You, Jude!" he roared. "What the hell you mean standing there talking to that no-account saddle bum? Git on that plow and git it goin'. I'll have no lazy son of mine idlin' away his time talking to every thievin' cowman that comes along." And to the rider, his arm outstretched, coiled whip in hand: "Git!"

The two-gun rider obviously was amused. He looked at the whiskey-flushed face and grinned. "Who's he, kid? Your old man?"

"My pa," Jude nodded, turning aside and moving to the plow handles.

"Looks to me like 'Pa' has done loaded himself up on panther juice and gone on the rampage. Son, you better do what he says. He looks terribly mad. Plumb riled up."

"Git!" Jude's father repeated fiercely. "If you think I'm afraid of them two pistols you're packin', I ain't."

"Most gents loaded to the tonsils with raw moonshine liquor generally ain't," observed the smiling rider. And to Jude: "Thanks for the tobacco, son. For the past week I've been smoking everything from ragweed to the bark off mesquite trees. Better get on the plow handles or he might take the hide off you."

"You bet I'll take the hide off him," the elder Gordon said. "Minute he gits to the house I'm goin' to teach him to waste time out here when there's work to be done. I'll do it now."

He snapped the length of whip out full and his arm went back. Jude unconsciously hunched his shoulders for the hide-cutting slash. But it didn't come. He turned for a look at his father. The upraised arm was slowly lowering the stock of the deadly blacksnake to the elder Gordon's side.

He was looking squarely down the muzzle of a heavy caliber pistol, held low at the rider's right hip.

"Just go ahead and do it, mister," came in a soft voice not at all in keeping with the rider's wild appearance. "I wouldn't make an orphan outa the kid, even though I'd be doing him a favor; but I'll fix up that arm and shoulder to where you'll have to learn how to work lefthanded. Give me the whip, mister."

"It's my whip . . . Blackie," Jude said, using the word hesitatingly and feeling a strange flush come to his face.

The rider sheathed the big pistol at his hip. "All right, son. It's your funeral. But if he uses that killer whip on you when it ain't even right to use it on a hoss, I'll just naturally come back here and give him a taste of it myself."

"It's all right. I can handle him, I guess," Jude said.

Blackie said, "That's all right, son," and watched as the broad back of the elder Gordon disappeared, striding angrily into the green forest of the tall corn. "How old are you?"

"Eighteen," Jude said.

"The hell! I figured you for about fifteen. Eighteen, eh? Well, when I was eighteen—and that was ten years ago—I taught my old man some manners with a singletree alongside the head and I haven't been back since. Guess I got to be going. Adios, and good luck."

"So long," Jude said, and then picked up the silver dollar.

He stood there between the plow handles, unwrapping the lines, his eyes on the broad back of the galloping horseman. So his name was Blackie and he wore two pistols. Jude wondered why. He turned to the team, taking hold of the lines and slipping them over a shoulder.

"You . . . Maud! Pete! Giddup! Gittyup!"

He finished the one furrow that afternoon, plowing south for two hundred yards to the corner, turning west along the ends of the rows, then north for a way, and finally into the easy turn.

Jude washed up at the bench inside the door and automatically began getting supper. His father would be in pretty soon, and his father always ate like a hog at a trough after imbibing an overload of whiskey. Somehow Jude didn't feel hungry . . . but there was still supper to cook. He lit the fire in the battered kitchen stove his mother had brought all the way from Missouri those many years ago and then looked into the oven. Some corn bread left over from dinner, a pot of beans sprinkled with chili he'd bought on the last long trip to Abilene. A couple of big steaks off the trail herd steer's haunches out in the smoke house, topped off by molasses, ought to suffice.

Footsteps sounded beyond the open kitchen door of the three-room shack and his father paused, resting a hand on the doorway to steady himself.

"I'm goin' to beat all holy hell out of you," he said thickly. "Talkin' to them cowpunchers and lettin' the weeds grow, eh? Stood right there while his own father had a pistol pulled on him. His own father? Your mother was no damned good, but I'll make a good man out of you if I have to beat you."

Jude had backed away into a corner. The old fear was upon him again, but for the first time he looked down in his hand and discovered that it contained a heavy skillet.

11

"You ain't going to whip me now or no more, Pap."

"All right, you young whelp! Defy me, will you? Defy me as the Israelites defied their God after they came out of Egypt. I'll put on you the same punishment that He put on them. I'll put the fear of the Lord God Almighty into you as He did in His wayward children. Where's that blacksnake? I'm going to take the hide off you."

He staggered toward the bedroom door and Jude, trembling with fear and anger, watched him go.

The elder Gordon was fumbling around in the other room, stumbling and cursing. Presently there came a half-muffled crash of the bed. Jude, the skillet in his hands, tiptoed to the door and looked in. His father was lying half across the bed.

Something like a sigh went out of Jude Gordon's young lungs. Slowly he lowered the half-ready skillet. His glance went from his father on the bed to the old Sharps Buffalo gun standing in a corner near his own bed. It was a .45-110-550. That meant a .45 caliber, 110 grains of black powder, and a 550-grain slug of lead. He had killed his first and only buffalo with that gun at the age of eleven, having to rest the huge, crow-bar-like barrel over a bank because he wasn't big enough nor strong enough to hold it up. The kick of it had almost torn off his shoulder. Later he had got to where he could fire it pretty good, leaning forward a bit and holding the stock tight against his shoulder. That way it didn't hurt him.

Jude went to his bed and put a knee on it, reaching up on a shelf he had built on the wall to keep his prized possessions. They weren't many. Eight or nine sacks of tobacco with papers, a few greenish-colored .50 caliber Sharps shells he'd picked up on the prairie—mementos of the buffalo hunters—several rattles of snakes he'd killed, including one with thirteen rattles or "rings" as he called them, a pocket knife with two broken blades, and a small rusty saw that one of the neighbors said was used to dehorn cattle. His books, or rather the books his mother had left him, were in a case along the wall, with a picture of her on top.

He took down the tobacco and the rattle with the thirteen "rings." You were supposed to handle the rattles very carefully because somebody had told him that they had a certain kind of dust on them and it would get on your hands and then into your eyes when you rubbed them and make you blind.

12

He went to the bookcase. There were so many he wanted to take, but it was one hundred fifty miles to Abilene and a man had to travel light when he was on foot. He chose two and placed them on the bed beside the tobacco sacks and the snake rattles. He picked up his mother's picture and put it with them. Then he took the skillet and went back into the kitchen, dropping it onto the top of the stove whose fire was still burning, down now to a bed of coals. He'd let the beans and corn bread stay in the oven. They would be hot when his father slept it off, and woke up hungry.

He made his way to the barn to get a gunnysack. Maud and Pete had finished their supper and were ambling around the lot, seeking a good place to stop and doze after the day's plowing. Jude found the sack, went over and rubbed each of them on the nose, and stood there looking about him. The sun was getting pretty low on the western horizon, losing its heat strength as it pushed downward, and the corn tassels were silent in the evening.

It didn't take long to pack his belongings. His mother's picture he carefully wrapped in a prized new shirt. He went into the bedroom again, after returning to the kitchen with the weighted sack. He had forgotten something. His eyes roved around the room until they caught sight of the hickory stock of the blacksnake whip beneath the edge of the bed. He brought it out, carefully coiled it, and put it in the sack. There were pencil and paper on his mother's writing desk and he sat down.

He wrote swiftly:

> Pa,
> *I'm going away to Abilene,*
> Jude.

That was all. He placed the sheet of foolscap on the bed where his father would be sure to see it when he came out of his stupor. Then he set out.

He covered three miles and then topped a ridge. Here he paused for a moment to ease the gunnysack to the other shoulder, and to look back. But the ridges of the undulating prairie, and the night, had swallowed up all that he had left behind. He drew in a deep breath of the night air, turned his young face to the north, and set out again. After a time he dropped down a long, scarcely definable slope, and saw in the darkness the waters of the creek ahead. From the distance, to his right, came the low, uneasy bawl of cattle, and he instinctively pushed his course a bit to the left.

He was three hundred yards from the creek when there came the sound of hoofs in the darkness and a man's voice called out sharply, "Speak up, mister. Who is it?"

Jude wanted to call out an answer, to give his name. But his tongue froze in his throat and he couldn't speak.

"Throw up your hands," came the command. "Get 'em up or I'll blow you to Kingdom Come."

Jude raised his hands as high as he could, the weight of the loaded gunnysack sending little streams of pain along his left arm. The rider came nearer. Jude saw the pistol in the right hand of the man in the saddle. He rode closer, peered down, and then suddenly he was laughing softly in the night.

"Hello, nester," Blackie said, sheathing that ominous big pistol at his right hip. "Well, I'll be damned," came chuckling softly through the night. "Kid, you had me nervous for a moment. Didn't know who you were. Where the devil are you going this time of night, out on the prairie?"

Jude lowered his hands and placed the gunnysack on the ground. "Abilene," he said.

He was shaking a little bit yet, the shock of frozen fear not yet passed.

"Abilene? What in the devil are you going to do there?"

"I don't know," Jude confessed honestly.

The rider in the night gave off with that soft laugh of his. It was the friendly laugh Jude recognized. He swung down.

"So you had it out with the old gent full of booze and carrying the bull whip? Good boy. But, kid, you can't walk one hundred and fifty miles across these prairies all by yourself. What's got into you anyhow? Don't you know the coyotes will get you?"

"I ain't afraid of the coyotes," Jude said. "I've lived here too long. And I'll get to Abilene."

The two-gun rider chuckled softly in the night. "I know you will. I knew you were a spunky little cuss the minute I laid eyes on you. But it's one hundred and fifty miles."

"I know," Jude said. "I've been there."

"What's it like?"

Blackie was rolling a cigarette—a quirly from the same sack Jude had given him that afternoon. Jude said, "It's a big town."

"Very good description. A very big town. Lots of people

14

there. That's what they said about Kansas City, Chicago, New York . . . the first time I went there. Lots of people. This is damned good tobacco—what did you say your name was?"

"Jude."

"Jude. Good name. And this is still good tobacco. I'm selfish, Jude. I hid it from the boys. Wouldn't dare roll a smoke when I rode in to camp for a change to a night horse. I got first trick tonight. Where you going now?"

"Down here by the creek to make a fire and cook."

The cigarette tip was glowing brightly in the darkness. It lit up Blackie's handsome face and even the long shaggy locks of his uncut hair. He pulled hard and the bright red tip described a glowing arc through the darkness as his hand dropped down to his side, near one of the guns at his hips.

Blackie put the cigarette to his lips again. "You'll do no such thing," he said. "You're coming to camp with me. I'll be relieved pretty soon and we'll go in and get supper. Come on, Jude. Get up back of me. Don't know whether this ornery broomtail will carry double or not, but it's a good time for him to learn."

They started out, and Blackie began to hum. Jude, sitting back of him, holding on to the concha straps of the saddle, could see the dark outlines of the bedded down herd not more than a quarter of a mile from Gramma Creek. Blackie's humming soon broke into words:

> Beat the drum slowly,
> And play the fife lowly,
> Play the dead march as you sing me a song. . . .

He coughed and Jude, his eyes on the dark outlines of the bedded down cattle again, said, "Why didn't you put them across the creek?"

"Huh?"

"The NP herd bedded down on the other side when they camped."

"Tell Shelby that. Nute would be happy to know it. If the NP bedded down over there, then Nute would be happy to know that *we* bedded down over here."

"It's going to rain tonight, Blackie," Jude said.

"All right. It's going to rain tonight. We had a lot of rains coming up from Texas."

"But these creeks fill up and come down. If it rains you'll

have a rising in no time. You shoulda bedded down on the other side."

"A weather prophet," Blackie said softly. "I'll tell Nute all about it. Maybe he'll roust out the herd and push 'em across tonight, because you say it's going to rain tonight and the creek is coming down."

"It'll come down fast. It always does when it rains," Jude insisted.

CHAPTER THREE

FROM SOMEWHERE off in the night came the sound of soft singing, a mournful song of life and lost love on the range. Blackie rode toward it, and presently a rider loomed up.

"My goodness, Blackie!" he exclaimed. "How fat you've got."

"Friend of mine behind me," Blackie's voice said. "How's the herd?"

"Quiet as a mouse. No trouble, thanks to the all high one. No more worry about stampedes from the NP outfit. Where'd you pick up the passenger? In the stagecoach business now?"

"Half a cent a mile. We give special service. Shut up! You talk too much anyhow. Baggage at no extra expense. He says it's going to rain."

"He *does?*" There was mockery in the tones. "Well, goodness gracious me . . . oh, my great-aunt Emma's left foot. I should have bought a new slicker instead of this leaky one I've used for five years. So it's going to rain? Look at the stars. That fool teacher of mine in school used to make us study the stars. He said that the one we were looking at might have been out for a million years and what we were seeing was just the glow of it as it went out. Tell the cook that when he blows out his lantern. It's going to rain. And me without a bath these last six months. Brrrrr."

Blackie's voice said, over his shoulder, "Don't mind him, Jude. His name is Mike Kessler. He reads a lot of books but none of them seem to show him how to win at bunkhouse poker. He's a poet at heart. That don't seem to help him either. You really think it's going to rain?"

"Yes," Jude Gordon said. "A real downpour, Blackie."

"The passenger weather prophet," Mike's voice said out of the darkness. "I tell you there is no accounting for the occult. I *knew* I should have got myself a new slicker and a weather-proof tarp for my bedroll. That old one of mine leaks like a sieve. You oughta hear the cook squall when I try to crowd the old bull out of from in under the chuckwagon. Well, run along, children. I must be away to me dee-uties."

Blackie gigged the black into motion and presently Mike was lost in the night. Jude could almost sense the grin on Blackie's face.

"Mike," his voice finally came over his shoulder, "is the scholar of the family. He can quote Shakespeare, poetry by the mile, and he's the biggest practical joker in the whole outfit. Watch out for him, Jude."

"I'll watch out for him," Jude said.

They continued their circle of the herd along the south edge, working eastward, and finally turned north. They rode up to the horse corral, where Jude slid down. Blackie descended with a long single step, and Jude saw then how the remuda corral was constructed. Stakes driven deep into the ground and a long line of ropes around it to keep the night horses in.

"This is the remuda corral, Jude," Blackie said. "We keep the night horses in here. Some horses just naturally are more sure-footed than others, and we use them for riding night herd. That's what you see in there."

"Where are the others?" Jude asked.

"The Negro night wrangler has them out, grazing. He'll bring them in about daylight, put them in the corral, eat breakfast, then turn in under a tree for the day to get his sleep in. When he wakes he'll straddle his hoss and burn the breeze to catch up with the outfit, following the trail made by the cattle."

He unloosed Jude's gunnysack from the saddle horn and handed it down. "You've got a lot of stuff there, Jude," he said. "Seems kind of heavy."

"Yes," Jude agreed. "I got a lot of stuff."

He stood and waited while Blackie unsaddled and turned the horse loose.

They came up to the fire and Blackie said, "Fine bunch of loafers."

"What's that you got with you—a stray maverick?" queried one, a buck-toothed, rather heavily built youth of about twenty-one, raising up on an elbow.

"That'll do for you, Grady," Blackie replied easily. "Just go back to your marbles and mumbledy-peg games."

That one brought a ripple of grins around the fire.

"Well," drawled the buck-toothed puncher, "I notice that he ain't wearin' no brand an' his ears ain't notched, but I reckon we can rope him in the mornin' and fix that up and then turn him loose with the herd. He'll soon git trail broke."

Jude had put down the sack, his face flaming at the laughter. He felt all sick inside and a kind of panic seized him. He picked up the sack in a sudden swift motion, flung it over a shoulder, but his bolt for freedom was stopped short by a powerful but friendly hand on his shoulder.

"Easy, Jude," Blackie's calm voice said. "I told you that some punchers are different from others—including talking too much. Grady's just a loud mouth who don't mean any harm. Come on back here and let's you and me eat supper. And if Grady opens his mouth again I'll push his boot in it."

Jude came back, his face redder than ever, all the hunger for supper having fled. He was too upset and uneasy at the strange position he found himself in: a "maverick."

A small, wiry man wearing an apron was at the chuck board in back of the huge chuckwagon. He had set out two plates with knives and forks.

"Come and git it," he said gruffly to Blackie. "I ain't got all night."

Jude and Blackie picked up the plates, Jude deliberately taking his last. He was going to watch Blackie and do what he did. He felt a close affinity to this man who had prevented his father from using the blacksnake bull whip on him that afternoon, and he somehow knew that Blackie held a special place all his own among the crew. Maybe it was because he wore two pistols instead of one; but Jude noticed that Grady had subsided. He lay back against his saddle, smoking a cigarette and looking at Jude and grinning in such a manner as to make him feel uncomfortable.

Blackie took his plate and went to the fire. Jude trailed him. He watched as the older man took beans, a big thick steak, and canned corn from the pots, after first pouring his tin cup full of coffee from the big black pot. He poured for Jude too and then went over to a vacant place near Jude's belongings and sat down cross-legged. He put the plate on his lap and began to eat. Jude did likewise, and with the first bite his hunger returned, gnawing at him as hunger never before had gnawed. For more than a year, since his mother's death, he had eaten his own cooking, except for the last trip to Abilene that spring.

Jude fought down his desire to eat faster and paced his bites to those of the big rider beside him. Conversation had picked up around the fire again. Nute Shelby sat with his back against the rear wheel of the wagon, on a goods box. He took little part in the general conversation unless directly spoken to; a sour-visaged, taciturn, hard man with a tremendous responsibility on his hands.

Far in the distance the lowing of the bedded down herd made an accompaniment for the conversation.

"So the NP is ahead of us, eh, Nute?" a middle-aged man with a bad bullet scar on the left cheek asked. Mike Kessler, the poet and joker of the outfit, had named him "Cicatrix" because of the scar, and it had been shortened to plain Cic.

"That's what the kid said," grunted the trail boss.

"What kid?"

"That one," with a sharp incline of the head toward Jude.

Again those critical eyes, a whole ring of them, swung to Jude, and he almost choked on his food. He lowered his head.

"You say they passed us day before yesterday, kid?" Cic asked pointedly.

"Yes," Jude said.

"Run over your crops?" Jude's clothes and mein proclaimed him a farmer. He couldn't have been anything else.

"No."

"He's sure a talkative cuss for a kid," Grady simply had to put in.

Blackie's head turned a trifle and his voice was a little cold as he looked at the buck-toothed puncher. "You shut up," he said in a matter of fact voice that had lost all tone. "Can't you see the kid's scared and uncomfortable? You open that mouth of yours at him just once more tonight and I'm going to shut it."

"None of that," Nute Shelby said, just as tonelessly.

"There'll be that and plenty more if Grady don't lay off this kid. And he's not as young as he looks. He's eighteen.

19

If it hadn't been for him we'd a missed Abilene by ten or fifteen miles. Now you shut up, Grady."

"Well," Grady defended himself in a somewhat mollified tone. "All I said was that he's some talkative cuss."

"He's got to make up for the too much talking you do."

Grady affected a bored yawn.

"I'd give a dollar for a good sack of tobacco right now," he announced.

Blackie put his empty plate aside and reached into a pocket of the torn shirt. The sack and papers went sailing through the air, landing near the buck-toothed puncher's booted feet. "Pay me," Blackie said.

Grady stared. "Where'd you git it?" he asked.

"Pay me," Blackie said.

"I—uh—"

Jeers rose in chorus. Grady, red-faced, reached into his pocket, brought out a silver dollar and, affecting nonchalance, tossed it through the light from the fire. It slapped into Blackie's palm and the two-gunman turned to Jude.

"Jude," he smiled, "I had an idea you'd make a pretty good cowpuncher, given time; but now I've changed my mind. You're going to become a merchant. Any man who can sell a sack of five-cent tobacco for two dollars ain't got any business poking cows up a loading chute. Here, Jude, take it."

"I already got a dollar you gave me and I don't need it. It's enough," Jude finished, feeling his face get red again.

Blackie forced the coin into his hand. The other men were listening and still grinning over Grady's discomfiture. Blackie made it worse by saying, "This kid gave me a sack of tobacco when I'd have given a dollar myself—without squirming like Grady's doing—and then wouldn't pick it up after I tossed it to him. Now he's got another. Jude, you're all right."

"Hell, Grady," spoke up another tobacco-hungry puncher, "ain't you going to give a man a smoke?"

Jude found courage to speak up then. His voice was high and off-key as he said, "He don't have to. I got some more."

He hurriedly reached behind him in the gunnysack. He brought out not eight or nine but thirteen sacks of tobacco with papers. He had had more than he thought. He shyly handed them to Blackie, and expectant grins broke out.

"This kid's all right," Blackie said, tossing sacks here and there. "And don't let me hear anybody calling him a kid any more. His name's Jude and that's what it's going to be. I hear one of you gents calling him a kid and I'll just naturally tangle with you. He's eighteen and that's man age in this country."

One of the punchers, opening his free sack, looked at Grady; and all of a sudden he burst out laughing. The laughter was contagious. It grew in volume, swelled higher, until even the brittle-faced Nute Shelby was grinning. Grady was a decidedly uncomfortable man at the moment.

Grady had to make a comeback somehow and he did it. He grinned in the face of the laughter, though back of the grin Jude saw cold anger and fury.

"Well, anyhow," the buck-toothed young puncher said, "as long as I've been without smokes it was worth it. But when I get to Abilene I'm sure going to drink me up a lot of whiskey. Ain't had a drink in nearly a month now and muh tongue is as dry as a dried cow. I'd give five dollars for a good drink of whiskey right now."

Jude innocently took the bait.

He reached back of him into the sack once more and brought out a one-gallon demijohn. "You don't have to do that," he said. "I kinda figgered you fellers might like a little and if I run into you it might come in handy. So I brought along some of Pa's best. Here it is."

Blackie started to say, "So that's why that sack was so heavy—" But he didn't quite make it. For a roar that shook the night went around the fire.

Jude sat there, astonishment on his face. He was bewildered and wondered if he had done anything wrong. He had only thought they might want a drink. He wasn't sure just what he ought to do now. He looked at Blackie appealingly. But Blackie was otherwise occupied. His head was bent over his chapped lap and his big shoulders were shaking convulsively. He leaned back and stretched out full length and his roars of laughter filled the night.

He struggled to a sitting position, wiped the tears from his eyes, and looked at Grady. That young man grinned sheepishly, almost foolishly, and again Jude caught that hidden threat back of his eyes. He knew he had made an enemy.

"Pay him," Blackie said. "You made your play and the kid backed it up with a royal flush. First he hunkered me, then he got Nute just as bad, now he's got you *twice* . . ." Blackie went off into laughter again.

21

Grady squirmed uncomfortably and looked at Nute. The trail boss said curtly, "The kid called your play. Pay him."

"I—uh—ain't got—Cic, will you lend me some money? Just till we get to Abilene and get paid off. I'm kinda short—"

"Not a danged cent," the scar-faced man cut in, still giggling. "You got yoreself into this mess and you sure as the devil can get yoreself out of it."

Jude mustered up his courage. "He don't have to pay anybody," he said. "It was Pa's likker and I guess I worked hard enough to earn it. I just brought it along in case—"

"He'll pay," Nute Shelby's curt, hard voice cut in. "You get five dollars out of Grady's wages when I pay off in Abilene."

"He don't owe me anything. Him or anybody else. Pa's got plenty of it and I brought it along. Anyhow, I won't get to Abilene for a few days yet."

Embarrassment held him again. He rose to his feet. The jug in Blackie's hands was tilted. He took a drink—a very small one, Jude noticed—and passed it on to the next man. It went the rounds of the fire, followed by a trip over to Nute, who curtly shook his head.

"Go ahead and drink up, boys, but when Pokey says roll out in the morning, you'd damn well better roll out. Any man who don't will get a rope wrapped around his bedroll and take a trip out across the prairie and one I'll guarantee he won't enjoy. Here, Pokey," to the cook.

Pokey wiped his lips and they gave off a smacking sound. He tilted the jug and long gurgles came from his throat. A man's voice said, "Save some for the night crew, you hawg."

Jude was up, and now he picked up his gunnysack with its precious belongings, including the coiled bull whip. "Well, I thank you for the supper," he said, "but I got to be going."

A man, raising the demijohn to his lips for a second time, slowly lowered it. "Going where, kid?" he asked in surprise.

"His name's Jude," Blackie's voice cut in very sharply.

"Where you going, Jude?" asked the man.

"I got to make camp over west of here," Jude explained awkwardly, unsure of himself. "It's going to rain tonight and I got to fix up a shelter in the willows. I'm obliged to you for the supper. I got some meat and stuff in the sack."

They were staring at him. This country kid's ignorance was beyond belief. This flatland farmer boy didn't know what it was all about. Leave them. After the tobacco and the jug of whiskey!

"Son," a very old puncher said in a soft and a very gentle voice, "you just put that sack right down. You're staying here with us. I've got an extra blanket in my soogan and maybe we can scrape up some more among the boys. Blackie says you're going to Abilene. So are we. You stay here."

"I'm much obliged but I wouldn't want to be beholden to nobody. I got enough meat and such stuff to last me till I get in. And him"—indicating Grady—"he don't owe me anything."

Blackie's voice broke the silence that followed; a stunned silence. This was a new one on them. This flatland farmer kid was all right. Blackie's words were directed at Nute Shelby.

"Nute, tomorrow morning you put this kid—you put Jude to work helping Pokey at the wagon. Give him an ax and let him chop down wood so's Peanut can haul it in on his rope." He turned to Jude. "The day wrangler has to help Pokey with the wood supply. You can cut it and Peanut can haul it in, and then you give Pokey a hand around the chuck-board. It's a lot better riding on the wagon than hitting it afoot. This Jude," he said to the others, "was walking a hundred and fifty miles to Abilene because his old man was going to cut him to pieces with a bull whip this afternoon."

Grady's voice, a touch of petulance in it, cut in from across the fire. "How'd you know, Blackie?"

"I threw a gun on him," came the cold reply; and then, for some strange reason, Blackie got up and walked alone into the night.

"Thanks," Jude said. "I'm much obliged to you, but I'll make out all right. And I expect I better get going down along the creek. I got to build a shelter before the rain sets in."

"Rain?" Grady was looking up at the sky and guffawing. "Look here, farmer, we learned all about rains and lightning and stampedes on this trip north. We got to where we know this prairie weather better than we know cows. It ain't goin' to rain."

Nute Shelby was looking at Jude. His penetrating eyes were sharp. "How come you know it's going to rain?" he demanded. And his eyes, too, went to the clear, starlit sky.

23

CHAPTER FOUR

RAIN SPLATTER upon canvas woke Jude. That and the sound of a man coming out of his bedroll. Nute Shelby. The foreman was up, jerking on his pants, his eyes seeking upward through the blackness of the night sky. It was overcast, heavy hung with clouds. Jude glanced at the horizon. It was black, pitch-black, and ominous-looking. In the distance the herd was no longer bellowing, it was bawling.

The first clap of thunder came, followed by more lightning. The bawl of the herd increased, a volume of sound that rolled toward them, engulfed them, and went on across the creek.

"Up!" Shelby's voice called. He was tugging on a boot now. "Roll out. The herd's going to break. Saddle and ride!"

They came out, grumbling and cursing. A man's voice said, "That nester kid was sure as hell right. He said it was going to rain. What he should hev said is that it's going to be a regular storm."

To Jude's surprise Pokey was coming out fast, reaching for his boots. Jude had thought they would stay beneath the wagon. He rolled out too.

"There come the cavvy," Pokey grunted. "Shore glad."

Jude could hear them: between fifty and one hundred horses coming in at a trot, the bell of the lead mare jangling plainly. The rain had increased. The big drops poured down, slapping off the canvas of the wagon and the tarp bedrolls.

"Get harnessed up, Pokey, and get that wagon across the creek before it rises," Nute Shelby yelled. "Hurry it up, men. Get back of that herd, and if it wants to stampede, send it north. We'll round 'em up later. Get going!"

They got going. Jude had never realized that men could move so fast. He saw scrambling cowpunchers rolling up tarp bedrolls and running toward the bedroll wagon. By now he was on his feet, his shoes with strings awkwardly tied, watching Pokey. The cook was grabbing up pots and pans and literally tossing them into the chuckwagon. Jude jumped in to give him a hand and in a matter of minutes Pokey was lifting up the hinged chuckboard and fastening it into place.

"The harness is all laid out in front of the wagon," Pokey bellowed. "Grab the two front bridles and I'll get the wheelers."

They ran for the front of the wagon. Horses by the dozen were milling around the remuda corral and a man was down by the opening, cursing while he worked at the rope knot on the gate. Men were saddling like mad. The sound of the bawling herd came louder. The remuda milled and Jude saw a black-faced rider: a Negro.

"They're going to stampede," called somebody's voice. "Let's roll, boys."

Jude found the bridles, laid out beyond the end of the wagon tongue. He grabbed them up.

"Which ones?" he called to Pokey as the two of them ran toward the corral. The Negro was spurring hard at a run around the outer circle of the milling remuda. Some of the "bunch quitters" were trying to get away. That was one of the tough jobs of a wrangler; the bane of his life was bunch quitters. As long as they knew you were watching them they'd stay put. But just let them get the idea you were loafing, taking things easy, and they'd start an unobtrusive graze off in the direction of the nearest gully. The Negro flashed past, a lean dark form in the saddle.

"Which ones?" Jude called again.

"That gray and black," the cook bellowed. "You can catch 'em with a bridle. I won't have a team I can't catch. Whoa, now, Gert! Stand still. Come here, you old fool! It's me. . . ."

Jude spotted the gray and called, "Whoa, boy," and started herding him in. But it was a storm and the gray wasn't going to be caught. Then, right over his head, a rope sang out and settled squarely over the recalcitrant one's head. The Negro hauled up, and even in the darkness, still split by lightning flashes, Jude could see his friendly grin.

"There you are, boy," called the night wrangler. "Take the rope offen his head and I'll git you the other."

Jude bridled with sure fingers and slipped off the noose. The Negro coiled his rope, and a wizened little man, also with bridles, called out, "Dam' you, Bugger, let the kid catch his and you try giving me a hand."

It was Joe, the crippled ex-puncher who drove the bedroll wagon.

Joe limped badly and couldn't get around much.

"Sure will, Mistuh Joe. Just a minute till I spot 'em."

Jude came out, leading the black and gray by the bridles. He trotted off toward the wagon, discovering to his surprise that Pokey already was there, harnessing fast.

Jude backed the team into place in front of the wheelers and was back to harness the second of them. He couldn't see Pokey's look of surprise in the night. Pokey had been boasting that he could harness a team faster than any man that ever walked.

"Look out for Gert on the right side," he called as Jude went in to hook the trace chains. "She'll kick the head off anybody but me."

She didn't kick Jude. He already was in between them, hooking the chains. The four stood strung out, ready to go. Pokey grabbed lines and went up over the hub of the left front wheel and Jude vaulted into the seat beside him. Off in the night came the drum of hoofs and that ominous bawling. Joe wasn't quite ready.

"Hurry it up," roared Pokey to the frantically limping little man. "We got to git acrost that crick and clear the herd or they'll be on top of us."

Joe hurled back a curse and Jude jumped from the seat, hitting the wet ground. He ran forward and ducked in, giving the bedroll wagon driver a hand.

"Let's go!" came the cook's bellowing voice.

Joe went up, taking the lines Jude handed him.

"Ridin' with me, kid?" he called down.

"I'll go with Pokey," Jude called, and ran back. He vaulted up again and Pokey's booted foot slashed hard at the iron brake handle, unlocking it.

"Git!" he bawled . . . and they "got."

The four-horse team hit the traces and the big chuckwagon lurched forward with a snap that threw Jude's head back.

"Git!" Pokey roared again.

They went out at a gallop, broke into a run, and Jude clung to the side of the seat, aware that this was the wildest ride a man ever took. Beside him Pokey sat with both legs braced, hauling and sawing at the lines while he peered through the rainy darkness.

They were heading due north, straight for the creek a quarter of a mile away. Pokey began shouting, "Whoa, now," and pulling back hard on the lines. But the running team were stretched out in full stride and wouldn't or didn't want to stop. The cook slapped on the brakes and the locked rear wheels slid through the mud and grass. The waters of the creek were just ahead.

Pokey got the panting team down to something resembling a trot and then released the brake again. Jude looked back. Joe, in the lighter bedroll wagon, was just back of them.

"Git!" Pokey bellowed. "Git on in there," slapping the lines down on their rumps.

But the horses that had been running but minutes before now displayed a strange disinclination to continue forward. The leaders were rearing and fighting the bits. Twenty feet ahead of them the dark waters of the creek lapped at the grass.

Pokey fought them and they almost got tangled up in the harness. "They won't cross," Pokey yelled. "The dam' fools have been through this before but they're still afraid of water. Git! Git! Gert, git out of it and come on across."

Jude leaned back, twisting around in the seat. His sack was just back of it. He brought out the coiled bull whip. Twenty feet of plaited leather.

He uncoiled it. Its twenty-foot length went out, trailing in the wet grass, and then it sang forward. He could make out the outlines of the horses' rumps in the night. Gert leaped forward and the others fell in. They hit the night waters of the rapidly rising creek, fighting and sloshing; and Jude coiled the blacksnake once more. Three minutes later they were across. The dripping team strained and struggled up the incline and Pokey, a look of astonishment on his face, wheeled them around on a rise and looked back.

In the night the rumble of a stampeding herd came above the roar of the storm.

"Almighty God!" the cook cried out. "They're running *south!* The boys couldn't turn 'em!"

CHAPTER FIVE

THE TEAM pulling the bedroll wagon had quite willingly followed the chuckwagon across the now turbulent waters. Jude had looked back and, in the light of the lightning flashes, could see it half floating, the water up above the floor bed. Those bedrolls, hastily flung in as their owners ran for the remuda corral, were soaking wet, he knew.

The wizened, crippled driver rocked up alongside of them, almost hub to hub. He hauled back on the lines.

"Wonder what time it is?" he called.

" 'Bout three o'clock," Pokey grunted. "Seems to me they broke kind of sudden."

"That's what I was thinkin'. Lord help them boys there. Son," this to Jude, "don't you ever get any fool ideas about becoming a cowpuncher. It's a dog's life."

Jude didn't answer. He sat in the pelting rain, wet all the way to the skin, listening. Far to the south the rumble of the running herd was broken by sharp, popping sounds.

"What's that?" he asked Pokey.

"Six-shooters. They're tryin' to turn 'em with gunfire. Sometimes it works and sometimes it don't. Well, let's make camp and get a fire goin'. The boys'll be stragglin' in pretty soon and'll want coffee and lots of it."

The huge chuckwagon lurched and went into motion toward a rise visible on the dark, wet horizon.

"Got to git clear of the crossin'," the cook explained to Jude. "Don't want no damn trail herd of three thousand steers runnin' over my camp."

They hauled up on the gentle rise, the bedroll wagon back of them. It was still raining. Jude jumped down and felt the wetness of the grass sink into his shoes.

"What'll we do with the team?" he asked, unhooking them.

"Unharness and put on hobbles," Pokey said. "I'll get 'em out of the wagon. The wranglers'll probably hold the remuda on the other side to give the boys fresh mounts. They can swim 'em across in the mornin'. Lord, what a night."

The little crippled man came over. He took off his streaming hat and wiped the rain from his face with a soaked sleeve.

"Hell of a night," he commented.

Pokey had taken a tarp and ropes from the wagon and was rigging a shelter from the left rear wheel.

"If you got an ax and a lantern handy I'll go try to cut and split some dry wood," Jude offered.

"No need to, son. I allus carry dried cow chips and some wood in the wagon for just such cases like this. Comes in handy on a roundup, in case of rain. Here . . . take this ax and drive in these iron stakes while I git the lantern lit."

They got the shelter rigged and the cook brought out a glass jug of kerosene. It seemed that the range-wise old Pokey was prepared for almost any emergency. In a matter of minutes the three of them were warming themselves over a fire blazing beneath the tarp shelter.

"The rain's lettin' up," Pokey finally said.

Gray dawn broke over a rolling, undulating prairie land, soaked to the core. The canvas on the two wagons drooped dispiritedly, heavy with moisture. A quarter of a mile south of them the flood creek waters rolled past, carrying debris and floating cottonwoods. Normally the creek was forty yards wide and three feet deep. It was one hundred and fifty yards of brown, swirling waters now.

Cattle, tired out from the run, began to straggle in sight on the south horizon. They gathered into miserable, bawling groups, and presently riders put in appearance. One of them was Blackie. He had a man in front of him in the saddle. They came to the creek's edge and Blackie slid off. He waded out into the stream while the other man sat drunkenly. The horse hesitated and then went in. Jude saw Blackie's hand on the horn, swimming alongside the horse, being carried downstream. But they got across without too much difficulty. They landed one hundred and fifty yards below the starting point and Blackie, his leather chaps soaked to sogginess, came on, leading the mount. He pulled up as the three men at the wagons went out to give him a hand.

They hauled the half conscious man out of the saddle and carried him to the shelter.

"Horse fell on him, huh?" Pokey asked.

"No," Blackie replied. "He's been shot."

"Shot! Who the hell did it? One of the boys trying to turn the steers?"

"It was no accident, Pokey. The herd was stampeded by riders waving slickers. God, that coffee smells good."

He poured himself a cup from the steaming pot while the cook went to work on the wounded man. The crippled little driver of the other wagon was over spreading soggy bedrolls all over the place. In a matter of hours the sun would come out, boiling hot. The sky was clear, the rain gone. Jude bustled about the wagon, helping the cook get breakfast. The Negro night wrangler and Peanut put the cavvy across shortly after sunup, after holding them across the creek the rest of the night. They were bunched on a hill two hundred yards away, the bunch quitters for once showing no inclination to wander off. Riders began to straggle in, wet, tired, and hungry. They ate in silence, changed horses, and swam back again to work the rapidly growing herd. At ten o'clock Nute Shelby rode up. He swung down and, like the others, went straight to the fire. His face was grim.

"Any missin'?" Pokey asked.

Pokey, like any chuckwagon cook, held a special place in the outfit. Any other man talking to the taciturn foreman at a time like this might have fared differently.

"Two hundred head, I reckon," Shelby said.

"How can you tell?" Jude asked.

The trail boss looked up from his plate and a smile came over his hard, practical face. "Well, it's like this, son," he said. "Some critters are marked differently. You got a brindle steer, a few big black ones, maybe, one with a slash of white along its flanks. You get to know them. I call 'em markers. We got about twenty head in this herd that we know by sight. Then when they stampede like they did and we round up, we start lookin' for markers. We got two missing. You can always figger that when a marker don't show up there's anywhere from fifty to a hundred head with him. Savvy?"

"Yessir," Jude said.

"They don't look like they're in a mind to cross," Pokey said. "All tired out, mad and bawlin'. You got a job cut out fer you, I'm thinkin'."

"We'll get 'em across," the trail boss said.

He rose from his haunches, placed plate and knife and fork in the big pan of water provided for that purpose, and went to his horse. He swung up and loped toward the distant remuda, his mount's hoofs throwing up mud gobs.

"There goes a good man," Joe remarked.

"Yah," Pokey replied. "A good cowman . . . and about as sociable as a Mexican fightin' cock. But he's all right."

It was decided to try to put the herd across about noon. The waters had subsided somewhat, but were still high. Riders were out on fresh horses, far to the south, scouring the country for the missing strays. They would hold the herd until the strays were found. They and one rider. A man named Webbly hadn't shown up.

Then, just before noon, he put in an appearance. He lay face down across another man's saddle. His horse too had been killed. The two of them had gone down in a futile effort to try to turn the madly running herd. Jude felt all queer inside when they brought him in and laid him out over by the chuckwagon tongue. He wasn't a day more than twenty-four.

Grady was eating near the fire. "What's the matter, farmer?" he jeered. "Never saw a dead man before?"

"You shut up," Pokey said.

"You go to hell," Grady said sourly. "I was a nester once myself and I'll talk all I damn please."

He swaggered over to the dirty dish pan, tossed in his plate and knife and fork, and mounted, heading for the cavvy and a fresh horse. Pokey said, "I never liked that big snot. Son, I got a grubbin' hoe and spade here. Maybe you better go up on the hill and start diggin' a grave for Webbly. Six feet long and three wide. I'll try to fix up a headboard with his name branded on it."

Jude took the implements and walked over toward the opposite slope, lying west of them. He dug for two hours, pausing now and then to wipe the sweat from his face. The sun was out, hot after the night storm. He looked down across the swell of the prairie. The creek was still up and for the last half-hour the riders had been trying to fight them across. But the herd had balked. Even the two great steers, leaders of the herd, refused to budge. They were tired, hungry, and angry. Jude got the grave down to four feet and went down to dinner. The body of Webbly, now covered with a canvas tarp, still lay where it had been placed. The wounded man smoked complacently, his right thigh bound in bandages made from washed flour sacks. The riders swam across by turns and ate hungrily.

The herd was at an impasse.

"Never saw 'em so damned stubborn," Pokey commented

31

to nobody in particular. "But that's a cow critter fer you. We git within a hundred and fifty miles of Abilene and they balk. Guess we'll have to wait until the crick goes down."

Jude spoke up from his plate. He was sitting alongside Blackie. "I can tell you how to get them across, I think."

There were seven men at the fire. Seven pairs of eyes swung and focused themselves on his young face. Nute Shelby paused over his plate.

"Yeah?" he said.

"It's what an old Indian once told me," Jude got out hurriedly and a little timidly. "They were driving two hundred head of Government-bought cattle to the reservation and run into a creek like this one."

Shelby had continued eating. He said nothing. Jude dropped his face to his plate.

"How did they do it, Jude?" Blackie's soft voice asked. "A man's never too old to learn. I never figured Indians as knowing more about cattle than cowpunchers, but then you never can tell. Me, I've got an open mind. It never hurts to listen."

"Well," Jude was talking directly to Blackie now, "it seems like when they wouldn't cross these Indians went down into the willows and cut a bunch of clubs. They beat the first bunch of lead steers across and the others followed right along. He said it was easy because the cattle didn't like to have those clubs bouncing off their heads. He was some kind of minor chief and spoke pretty good English. Lots of them come by our place," he added.

Blackie's face lifted. His eyes met those of Nute Shelby. He said, "Well, Nute?"

"I'm still running the outfit, Blackie. We'll put 'em across after dinner. They get hungry enough from being bunched and they'll cross."

Jude got up and put away his eating utensils. "I guess I better get back to the digging," he said to Blackie. "I'm down four feet now."

Shelby's voice came from across the fire. "That's deep enough so's the coyotes won't get him. Don't waste any more time. We've got more important things to think of. You and Joe pack him up there, kid. Soon's we get the herd across I'll hold burial services and we'll get on our way."

They changed horses again and went back across the still swiftly runing waters. Jude, under Pokey's direction, took an ax and went west, past the grave, into the mesquites. He began cutting and piling wood. An hour later Peanut rode up. Peanut was sixty if he was a day, and though Jude had no way of knowing it Peanut had watched Major-General Jeb Stuart receive his mortal wound at Yellow Tavern in the wild fight with Sheridan's cavalry.

"How are you-all, son?" the wrangler asked, reining up.

"Pretty good," Jude said. "How are they making out with the cattle?"

Peanut was taking down his rope, building a large loop in his small but powerful hands. He shook it out until its spread touched the ground.

"Ah reckon they ain't," he said. "Crittuhs can be powerful ornery sometimes. Heah. Put this heah rope around 'bout ten of them sticks theah and ah'll drag 'em ovuh to the wagon. Nevuh see sech a belly achuh as thet Pokey. He worries moah about wood than ah do about who lost the Wahr Between the States. I'll send that nigguh Buggah ovah fo' the rest. It ain't his job, him bein' the night wrangler, but I brought that nigguh west with me when he wasn't moah'n a pickaninny an' he'll jump when ah pop the whip."

Jude took the loop and fastened it around enough of the dry wood to make a good load. Peanut turned, dallying around the saddle horn. The rope tightened and the cow horse, straining away, moved toward the chuckwagon with the load dragging away behind. Twenty minutes later the Negro youth came loping up. He gave Jude a friendly grin.

"How you makin' out, boy?" he asked.

"Pretty good. Peanut said he'd send you over. You want me to loop up this wood?"

"That Peanut. Now there's a man fo' you." Bugger was swinging down. "Nobody around this camp knows it, but my mammy and pappy wuz slaves of his family down in Gawgia until Mistuh Lincoln freed 'em. Peanut's real name is Cunnel Edward Sutherworth. But that country sho' was in bad shape after the wahr. So the cunnel stuck around fo' a few years an' finally he ups and decides to come out West. He tol' my mammy and pappy. 'You's freed now, but ah'll take this Bugger with me out West,' so heah we is. We been rovin' 'round the country evuh since, me an' the cunnel, which is how come ah turned up as night wranglah on this heah outfit. Cunnel got me the job."

He was smoking a cigarette from the tobacco Jude had given the men, bending to loop the rope. He pulled it up tight around the last of the wood and swung up again, strong and lithe in the saddle. He looked down at Jude.

"Heah come Grady. Wonder whut he wants? Look heah, white boy, don't you say nuthin' about what I tol' you about the cunnel bein' a cunnel. He's Peanut, an' nobody asts questions about who a man is or wheah he com fum."

"I understand," Jude said.

"Fine. Cunnel knew I tol' you that an' he'd skin my black hide right off my black backside."

CHAPTER SIX

GRADY REINED up and looked down at Jude. "Gimme that ax, farmer, and be quick about it."

Jude stared back at the bigger youth. He didn't like Grady at all; he liked him less and less every time they met.

"I ain't keeping it from you," he said. "There it is."

"Hand it up here."

"You were sent up to get it. I ain't keeping you from it."

Bugger rocked in the saddle. "Wha-wha-wha!" he roared with laughter, slapping his thigh. "That li'l ol' farmer boy he sho' done tol' you where to head in. 'I ain't keepin' you-all fum it,' he says. *Wha-wha-wha!*"

Grady turned on him fiercely. "You shut yore dirty mouth."

"You gits funny with me an' Peanut'll just nat'ully blow yo' haid right off. You-all'd look funny walkin' around widout a head. Just like a dawg-goned chicken whut got it chopped off fo' the Sunday dinner."

Grady snarled at him again and rode over, bending from the saddle. He almost made it, fumbling on the ground, and then had to dismount to pick up the implement.

"If you wasn't just a tramp maverick I'd beat yore head off," he sneered. "An' I think I'll do it anyhow when we git to Abilene."

"I expect," Jude said, "that one reason you're bluffing is because of what Blackie would do to you. But don't worry, I won't let him take a hand. So you can take off that gunbelt any time."

"I ain't got time. Nute wants this ax. But I'll get you yet." Grady wheeled and loped away, down toward the creek.

Bugger was grinning like a black gargoyle. "I sho' wish he'da called yo' booger, boy. Dawggoned if ah don't think you-all could give 'im a round or two."

He leaned his hard, lithe black body to one side and let the rope tighten. The wood began to move on its way to Pokey's domain.

Jude stood watching as the jogging horse passed the bed-roll wagon, coming up, Joe had hooked up the team, put the dead man into his bedroll, and was bringing him up. He hauled up beside the grave and found Jude waiting. Joe got limpingly down and went around to the back, letting down the tail gate.

"We might as well leave him in outa the sun until Nute and the boys get here," he said. "And that might be quite a while, from the looks of things. Nothing to do but wait."

He sat down in the shade of the wagon and removed his hat to reveal a bald head, then rolled a smoke. Jude rolled one too, his eyes on the distant herd. Grady was back across now and Jude saw Nute Shelby waving his hands toward the willows. The buck-toothed, foul-mouthed puncher swung down near a screen of willows and began to slash away. Fifteen minutes later he had several clubs about four feet in length and from an inch to two inches in diameter. Riders rode up and each took a club. They spurred into the head of the herd and the clubs began to thud off red hides and bounce off backs and noses. A new note rose in the distant bawling. Three riders rushed a small group, and under a hail of blows the steers broke. They pushed out into the stream and began to swin. The clubs flailed anew and more followed.

The herd was on its way across.

Joe sat there watching the dripping twenty-eight hundred lumber by nearly a mile to the east. He said, "Well, I'll be damned. Now I've seen everything. And me workin' cattle since we started rounding up unbranded mavericks right after the close of the War."

Five of the riders broke away from the herd and galloped to the chuckwagon. Jude could see Nute Shelby talking to Pokey from the saddle. He was gesticulating. Pokey handed him something from the wagon and then the trail boss turned toward one of the men and again said something: an order of some kind. The rider—it was Grady—started loping toward the four hobbled chuckwagon mounts grazing some distance to the north.

"We're movin' out," Joe announced. "Here comes Nute and Blackie and Cic and Mike. Guess that's the buryin' party." He rose to his feet and put on his hat.

The four riders came up at a fast trot and swung down. Nute Shelby looked at Jude strangely and said nothing. He rapped out to Joe, "Get him out of there and into the ground, Joe. We've lost more than a halfday and got to get rolling."

Jude sprang to the back and together he and the limping little man carried the tarp-covered figure in its blankets and lowered it into the hole. The men gathered around and the trail boss took a Bible from his belt where it had been shoved down inside against his stomach.

He read a very short burial service, closed the book, and looked at the others, putting on his hat. "Blackie, you and the boys get back to the herd. Jude, you fill in this grave with the shovel. Joe, get rolling and load up them bedrolls and the ropes and stuff for the corral. Pokey's getting ready to hitch up. Get that grave filled in as soon as you can, Jude; then go down and give Pokey a hand. That's all, boys."

In two minutes Jude was left alone. He went to work, filling in the shallow grave, and trying his best to make the mount neat and uniform. He picked up the tools and made his way down to the wagon. Pokey already was hooked up and loaded.

"All right, Jude, let's roll," the cook said. "Climb up, son."

Jude went up over the hub and Pokey said, "Here, hold this."

It was a small board from a precious pile he kept for kindling, made from a goods box. On it, burned with a heated iron stake, were the words: *Webbly, from Texas.*

That was all. They stopped at the grave long enough to put it at the head, Pokey yelled, "Git!" and they went out at a fast trot.

CHAPTER SEVEN

Nute Shelby rode with Blackie at point when they first sighted Abilene in the distance, miles away across the flat prairie. The foreman was more worried than he cared to admit. He wasn't just quite sure what the next move would be. Reports had drifted down the trail that you didn't have to worry about cars; there were plenty. And buyers aplenty too. "Takes a lot of time to load a herd," Blackie commented. "Jude saw two go by within a week. No telling how many more were coming in from other directions. Five of what you owe me gets you one of what the old man is going to get out of this herd that's the NP outfit over there, waiting for cars. Ten more of what I've got coming says those two hundred lost head will turn up here with our T34 brand on their hides. Want to bet?"

"Maybe they rebranded," grunted Shelby.

"Who?"

"Rustlers. Never heard of rustlers working close to a shipping point, but anything can happen in this business. They could rebrand and run in with another herd."

"They were two days ahead of us. And we lost hours until that nester kid showed us how to get across Gramma Creek."

"I know."

The answer was short, typical of the trail boss. The loss of those two hundred cattle was a sore spot with him. He lived for cattle. He'd been entrusted with three thousand prime steers and he was showing up with a two-hundred-head shortage.

"If I could get a look at some of that NP stuff and see any signs of fresh rebranding," Blackie said, "it wouldn't be much trouble to shoot a steer and skin it. Our old T4 brand would show beneath the hide."

"And have a fight on our hands? Not in this town. Wild Bill Hickock is marshal, and from what I hear he's a bad man to tangle with. Don't you worry about the two hundred head. We'll have a few days and I'm keeping my eyes open. I got a

37

hunch they'll show up. Well, I'd better go over and tell Pokey where to put the wagon. Grass looks good two miles east of here. We'll try it anyhow. Tell the wing men to start swinging them. Get the leaders over."

He rode off at a gallop. Blackie turned in the saddle and threw up his hand in signal to the right wing man on the east side. Blackie turned to the west, the big steers now acknowledged as leaders instinctively following the horse. The right wing man had taken down his coiled rope from the saddle. He doubled it and began whacking steers on their lean rumps.

"Ho-ho-ho!" he called, striking right and left at the bobbing rumps. The bellows increased, but the head of that long line of steers, sinuous like the curve of a snake's body, swung to the west. They plodded on.

Nute Shelby pulled up alongside the right front wheel of the wagon.

"There she is, boss," Pokey called down. "And it looks like we got visitors."

"Looks that way," grunted the trail boss.

"Cattle buyers," Jude said to Pokey. "They'll be on you like bees."

"We're turning the herd," Shelby said, working his horse in close to the lumbering four-horse chuckwagon. "Swing over and camp somewhere about two miles west of that other herd over there. Fix supper for about six men. The rest of the boys will be eating in town, I reckon."

"Aw, hell, Nute," Pokey protested. "Let 'em get their own supper tonight. I got business in town."

The riders, three of them, were now but a hundred yards away; men in city clothes and the kind of stovepipe hats Lincoln had worn. Jude, sitting in the seat beside the cook, wondered how a man could keep one of those hats straight while riding at a gallop. Strung out on the plain back of them were two more groups. More cattle buyers. The trail boss's confidence suddenly took an upsurge.

But he was still Shelby, the man who had brought them through. He said, "That's too dam' bad, Pokey, but some of the boys have got to hold this herd. Everybody can't go into town."

The first of the group of buyers came up. He was a florid-faced man with long dark sideburns on his cheeks.

"Pardon me, sir," he said. "But where can I find the man in charge of this herd?"

38

"You're looking at him," Nute Shelby said curtly.

"Glad to meet you, sir. My name's Willoughby. I represent the Willoughby Cattle Company. Shippers, you know. I'd like to buy this herd. Every hoof. And we pay cash."

He named a price that left the trail boss's mouth slightly open. Shelby cleared his throat. Twenty-eight hundred head at . . .

"Tell him not to take it," Jude's voice said. "He can get more."

He had intended it as a whisper to Pokey. But the words had carried. Other men in derby and beaver hats were coming up. Shelby hesitated.

"Hold it, sir," cried out a man topped by a beaver. "I'm prepared to pay you more."

The third came up. "Gentlemen," he cried, and this appeared to be directed at Shelby and Pokey and Jude as well. "I have a full crew of men to take charge of this herd, if you'll sell it to me. . . ."

Jude saw the trail boss relax suddenly. He almost lounged in the saddle. Three men began to bid. The last man to arrive was short and wiry. His presence seemed to be resented by the others.

"I've got a full crew of men to take over this herd, sir," he cried to Shelby. "I'll pay on the hoof according to your count. Cash on the barrel head."

Nute Shelby ignored him. He turned to Pokey. "Maybe," he said in the softest voice Jude had ever heard him use, "you won't have to fix supper after all, Pokey." And to the man: "Mister, you've just bought yourself about twenty-eight hundred head of Texas cattle. Get your crew out here and take over."

"Thank you, sir. My company pays the highest prices."

"This time. Maybe not next time." And to the two unsuccessful bidders: "Sorry, men. The herd's sold." And again to the buyer: "That's the herd and nothing else. The cavvy and wagons stay with the outfit."

"All yours, mister."

The man who had just bought the herd loped away, followed by the others at a disgruntled trot. Pokey licked his lips. "I'll put the wagon in close to town so's in case the boys want any grub it'll be handy."

A fleeting grin crossed the trail boss's pleased face. "I can imagine," he said, "about how much cooking *you'll* be doing."

39

CHAPTER EIGHT

THE TRAIL boss sat at a small table, a kind of tally book in front of him. Beside it was piled more money than Jude had ever thought existed. The ragged riders, fifteen of them, were crowded around, their eyes bright with eagerness and expectation. As each man was paid off he hurried out.

Jude stood waiting. He didn't know why he should be there, but Blackie had insisted. He shifted to the other foot, feeling green and out of place.

One by one the riders received their pay and left. Blackie tucked the money into his ragged pants pocket and came over as Bugger and Peanut went forward to be paid off.

"Smoke, Jude?" the two-gun rider asked.

Jude nodded. He smoked and watched Peanut and Bugger file out. Then, to his astonishment, he heard his name called.

Shelby looked up over the still considerable pile of money in front of him. "I got you down for one hundred dollars," he said curtly. "Here it is."

Jude stared at him, started to demur. But the foreman already had dismissed the matter with a curt nod, making notations in the black tally book.

Blackie's voice said, "Take it, Jude. You earned it in a lot of ways. He wouldn't be paying you unless he figgered you're worth it. Don't forget the five out of Grady's for the liquor," he added.

"I'd forgotten," grunted Shelby, and handed over the money. He lifted his hard eyes to Jude's face. His voice, when he spoke again, was a little softer. "You can go back to Texas with us if you want to, son. The outfit will be leaving in a few days, depending upon a number of things. It's not an easy life on the T4. Thirty dollars a month, for you, working from daylight until darkness, and sometimes longer than that. Hot in summer and so cold in the winter it'll cut you like a knife. Cattle as wild as antelopes and a damn sight meaner. But if you're fool enough to want to make a cowpuncher, then, by God, we'll make a cowpuncher out of you."

It was, Jude thought, the nearest thing to real humanity Shelby had ever displayed.

"I'll go," Jude said. "I'll try to earn my pay."

"You'll earn it. If you don't, I'll fire you damned quick."

"Come on, Jude," Blackie said. "If you're going to become a cowhand, you'll have to get ouifitted. Let's go."

Jude picked up his belongings in the sack and they went out in the hallway and descended the steps. At the desk Blackie stopped. "I want a room for two," he told the clerk.

Jude put his belongings in a corner of their hotel room, locked the door, and the two of them descended into the street. "First place is a barber shop," Blackie told him. "Always keep up appearances, Jude. It pays. Take care of your equipment, and buy only the best."

He started to say something else and then Jude sensed the stiffening of Blackie's lean, whipcord body. Four tough-looking men were approaching along the boardwalk, led by a big dark-faced man. Blackie stopped and Jude saw that his hands lay close to the two heavy guns at his hips.

"Hello, Harrison," he said insolently. "How's the cow stealing business these days?"

The big man stopped abruptly, his eyes narrowing. The men back of him had stopped too. They looked like nesters to Jude; yet there was something in their appearance, the guns they wore, that proclaimed them men who could ride.

"I don't want any trouble with you, Blackie," Harrison said. "And you wouldn't try making it if you didn't know that Hickock is out of town for a few days."

"Sold your stolen herd yet?"

"I don't like that kind of talk," Harrison said harshly. "There are four of us here."

"You better go back and get some more help," sneered Blackie.

"I don't want any trouble," Harrison repeated.

"We lost Webbly back at Gramma Creek," Blackie said. "Somebody rattled a slicker and stampeded them again. Tolson got shot. If I ever get any proof of what I think I'm going to kill you. Come on, Jude."

They passed warily, like strange dogs ready to snap. Blackie didn't look back. That much contempt he showed them.

"Who's he?" Jude asked.

"Harrison. Head of the NP outfit."

41

"Another ranch?"

There was a saloon's inviting doors in front of them and Blackie pushed in. They leaned against the bar, waiting for the busy man behind it to take notice of them.

"No," Blackie said. "NP means Nester Pool. You see, Jude, down in our country the nesters are coming in. Most people look upon the big cow outfits as a bunch of greedy range hogs pushing out the farmers. Nobody thinks anything of a nester stealing and butchering a steer now and then. All the big owners expect it, including Travers, who owns the T4. But this gang of nesters did things a little differently. They organized, with Harrison leading them. He claims to be a farmer. He's got a few acres of land down along the edge of the shinery. But from the time Harrison came in organized stealing began. The nesters banded together and began raiding up right and left. They'd even wait until it rained hard and then shoot a cow and let her float downstream, picking up her calf and rebranding. When they got enough they formed what they called the Nester Pool, the NP brand, and drove north. Fifteen hundred head, and every one of them stolen."

The barkeep moved toward them, making perfunctory swipes at the polished surface with a foul-smelling, wet bar rag. His eyes looked a question.

"Old Overalls," Blackie said.

The barkeep nodded, reached back of him, and placed two glasses and a quart bottle of Old Overholt whiskey. He shot Jude a questioning glance.

"My son," Blackie said, interpreting it, and pouring. "My youngest of four sons. The others ran away from home when they were three and became pirates."

He placed the bottle beside Jude's glass, indicating that Jude could drink or not, just as he chose. Jude poured.

"You sure you can take it?" Blackie grinned.

"Yes."

"I forgot. Your old man makes stuff stronger than this. My mistake, Jude. Drink up, have another, and we'll go take care of some business. I have a lot of it."

They drank, had another, and went out. Blackie headed for a store. They went inside into a structure that was long and dark and the shelves of which were loaded with almost every type of goods. Jude fingered the money in his pocket.

They bought. They came out into the street again with their arms filled with packages. Next door was a gun shop. Blackie fumbled for the door knob, found it below the packages in his arms, and they entered. They put packages on the counter. A man in a canvas apron came forward.

"Gentlemen?" he inquired.

"Thank you very much," Blackie replied. "A man of my age and as ragged as I am seldom gets such compliments any more." He slid the heavy pistol at his right thigh from the sheath and deftly punched out the five loads from the cylinder, the big cartridges thudding to the counter. One chamber was empty; the one beneath the hammer. Jude also noticed that the front sight was filed off. Blackie said to the gun shop proprietor, "She seems a little bit too easy on the trigger. I want you to touch up the notch just a bit and increase the pull by about a pound."

The man took the gun in experienced hands and reached for a small weight beneath the counter. It had a hook on it. He cocked the gun and placed the hook inside the trigger guard, lifting it gently. The hammer fell. The man looked at Blackie and nodded.

"You're right, sir. A bit worn in the notches. I can take care of it. How about the other one?"

"The other one," Blackie said softly, "is going to stay right where it is until I get that one back."

"I understand, sir. I can take care of this in a few minutes, if you care to wait."

"We forgot the barbershop. We'll be back."

They went out. There was a barbershop next door. Blackie was humming. They went in and sat down in chairs and the obsequious barbers got busy. The scissors went to work and locks of long hair fell to the floor. Jude indulged in the luxury of having his fuzz scraped clean, his first shave in a barbershop. He looked over at Blackie in the next chair. What had emerged from beneath those long black, shaggy locks was one of the handsomest men Jude had ever laid eyes on.

"You like the job, sir?" inquired the barber.

Blackie said to his reflection in the mirror, "What a handsome son you are. Come on, Jude," and they left.

They went back to the gun shop next door. The smith had the gun apart and was working. They went over to a rack of new repeaters, and Blackie took one down. He examined it critically.

".44-40. Try it, Jude. Not much for range but a good handy saddle gun. Ever shoot a rifle?"

"A little," Jude admitted, working the new action. The lever flowed free under his strong, sure hands. This was a lot different from the old Sharps single shot.

"Put it on the counter. It's yours."

They went to the revolver rack next. Blackie slid out three or four guns, put them back, and finally turned with one in his hands. He looked at Jude. "If you're going back with us, pardner, you'd better take one of these with you. They come in handy sometimes. Unless I miss my guess we've got a first-class range war on our hands. Harrison is too well organized and has got by too easy to stop his nester rustling. That is," he added, "unless I shoot him dead before we leave Abilene."

Blackie laid the new .44 Colt on the counter and waited until the gunsmith had returned his weapon. He tested the trigger action again, found it to his liking, and handed over the other gun. This one was all right. He slipped it into the left-hand sheath and picked up the new weapon.

"File off the front sight," he ordered. "If Jude ever gets into a lead-throwing fracas I don't want him going down because his gun snagged in the holster. Savvy?"

"Yessir, I certainly do."

They returned to their hotel room loaded down with purchases.

"Now for a good hot bath," Blackie said.

They took one in the hotel's bathroom, scrubbing themselves furiously. Blackie was singing in the bathtub.

Oh, Myrtle got drunk at the dance,
Oh, Myrtle got drunk at the dance,
She went to Laredo to get a new hair-do,
But Myrtle got drunk at the dance. . . .

"I never heard that song before," Jude said.

"Neither did anybody else. I made it up by myself. Jude, we're going to tear up this town tonight. I got a girl here. She was a singer in Kansas City shows but she's here now. I wrote her from the ranch and told her we were on our way with the herd. She said she'd be here. Maybe she's got a friend."

Jude felt himself blushing and Blackie, up to his neck in soapy water, laughed.

"Jude, you're all right. Yee-hoo! I'm going to kill a man tonight and then make love to the prettiest girl in Abilene."

CHAPTER NINE

BLACKIE AND JUDE went into a bar and had another drink. Blackie wasn't drunk but he was "high" and feeling his oats.

"Jude, you sure can handle this stuff. I know, your old man runs a corn still. You're taking me drink for drink and it's showing no effect on you. Let's have another before we eat. This is my night to howl."

Jude drank with him. The bar was fully sixty feet long. It was lined with riders from everywhere; bull whackers; buffalo hunters now turned bone pickers. Four men came in —Harrison and his three followers. The big man bellied up to the bar, shoving men aside. He wore two guns. A "nester" who wore two guns.

Blackie said, "Wait a minute, Jude," and made his way along the bar. He stopped twenty feet farther along, leaving Harrison and his three dog tails between him and Jude.

"I got a bad taste in my mouth," Blackie's voice came, distinctively and insultingly. "Give me an Overalls to cut it."

He was leaning with his left elbow on the bar. And he wasn't looking at the bartender; he was looking at Harrison.

"We lost two hundred head at Gramma Creek," he grinned at the bigger man. He was bedeviling him, sneering at him. Jude felt it and he tensed. Harrison and his three men were rigid, waiting. "Stampede. Webbly got killed and Tolson got shot. I've been up and down the street and I haven't seen but four of your boys. Maybe they're across the tracks in the bawdy houses—where they belong—and maybe it's just a coincidence that they're not in town."

Grady came in. He had bought himself a new outfit, and he was half drunk. He leaned up beside Jude at the bar.

"I'll buy you a drink before I whip hell out of you, farmer," he said, his eyes on Jude's new wide-brimmed hat, blue flannel shirt, trousers and boots.

"Get out of my way," Jude said, his eyes on Harrison's right hand.

The bartender came over, giving Grady the expectant look that bartenders give to a new customer. "Whiskey, single," Grady grunted. "This damned farmer is too good to drink with me because he's a pal of the T4 outfit's two-gunman."

"Get out of my way," Jude repeated.

Blackie was saying, "Those two hundred head will turn up. I hope they do."

He picked up his drink to down it and in that instant Harrison drew his right-hand pistol. It came out fast. But Jude had somehow expected it and already had flicked the coils of the bull whip off his shoulder, laying them out on the floor in a twenty-foot length of plaited leather. Harrison's hand was half up out of the sheath, holding the gun, when the popper sang out. Blackie's drink was coming down from his lips.

Harrison let out a yell of pain and a gun clattered to the floor. He grabbed his right hand, a red welt appearing as if by magic across the knuckles. Blackie had acted automatically. In a flash his two pistols were out covering the others.

"You dogs," he said, grinning. "You yellow dogs."

"Here . . . here!" broke in the sweating bartender. "Cut it out, you Texans. Do your fighting outside."

Nute Shelby's tall figure broke through the swinging door. "Cut it, Blackie," the trail boss's voice said. He moved forward. "Get out of here."

"I'll get out when I'm damned good and ready," Blackie replied, ignoring the foreman. Then he calmly shoved the guns into their sheaths. "There were four of you this afternoon. There still are. Now throw 'em."

Two men wearing town marshals' badges converged, shouldering their way between the two groups. "All right, Texans. No fighting. Do it when you get back home."

"There won't be any fighting," Shelby's voice said calmly. "They're my men and I give the orders. Blackie, you and Jude get out of here. Harrison, you stand pat until they leave."

Jude was coiling the blacksnake. It was over. Grady stood with his drink half poised. Jude and Blackie went out.

"I'd have shot it out with the four of them," Blackie said.

"I know you would have."

"Thanks for the play, Jude. You're pretty handy with that bull whip. I'm glad you brought it along. Let's go eat."

Jude was still filled with a strange kind of keyed up excitement, and he wondered how this handsome man beside him could dismiss such a matter with a laugh. They went down the street. They ate in a café and Jude left the whip at a saddle shop to have it fitted with a new popper and some spares, promising to return the next day. He still had to buy a tarp bedroll and a saddle.

They walked down the street, full and contented, and with Jude feeling a bit awkward in his new boots. They didn't hurt; he simply wasn't used to the high heels. He felt a foot taller.

"Let's go across the tracks," his older companion said. "I told you I've got business."

They went across the tracks. Here the buildings were about the same, with a curving street serving as thoroughfare for the saloons, gambling dives, and bawdy houses. On one corner stood a huge place of two stories.

"That's the Prairie Dove," Blackie said. "Bartender told me. And she's singing there, he said."

"I've seen it," Jude said. "I've never been in it."

"We're going in now."

They crossed the dirt street and came up on the board sidewalk and pushed inside into a mass of bright lights. A bar at least one hundred feet long was lined, and the gaming tables at the opposite side of the room, were crowded. At the far end was a stage, with a five-piece orchestra playing in a pit. Two men in derby hats were dancing, their checkered suits showing up garishly against the raiment of the crowd. Those at the gaming tables were paying no attention. Those drinking at the tables were. Jude followed Blackie back along the length of the bar and took position alongside him against the wall. Blackie's eyes were not upon the performers. Their glittering depths were searching the crowd.

"No NP men here," he finally grunted. "I'd bet a hundred dollars of the wages I've got that the rest of them are out with that two hundred head we lost."

He shifted his attention to the stage, relaxing a little. Six girls were out, dancing a sort of cancan.

"That barkeep said she'd be here," Blackie said.

When the number ended a man with a spit curl in his parted hair and sporting a long black mustache came out.

47

"La-dees an' Gen'lm'n," he bawled above the buzzing uproar. "Our chief attraction at the Prairie Dove, direct here from the East, the young su-prano of su-perior qualities, your favorite of the prairies, Miss Edwina Cochran."

"Here she comes," Blackie said in an aside to Jude.

She came out, golden-haired and in a long flowing dress, with enough shoulders bared to be considered daring; just about the prettiest thing Jude had ever seen. She sang three songs, then retired.

"Come on, Jude," Blackie said, moving away from the wall.

"Maybe I'd better stay here," Jude said, embarrassed. "You can come on back to the hotel room when you're ready."

Blackie's devil black eyes were dancing. "Lord, how naive you are, Jude," he laughed. "I'm not coming back to the hotel tonight. Neither are you. Come on."

They pushed their way in among the tables and made for a curtained doorway at the left side of the stage. In the wings a man in a derby hat saw them. He bustled forward authoritatively.

"Here . . . you cowpunchers," he snapped out brusquely. "Nobody's allowed backstage."

Blackie's strong hands reached out, gripping the edge of the cast-iron hat. He pulled down hard. The owner's eyes and part of his face disappeared into the hard crown.

He walked on through, into a flurry of girls and acrobats and comedians. Two belligerent stagehands came forward, saw the two guns, and stopped.

"Who you lookin' for, cowpunch?" one asked.

"I'm not a cowpunch," Blackie sneered. "I'm a gentleman rider of the open ranges of Texas and this is my gentleman friend. Where's Edwina?"

"Miss Cochran? It's against the rules—"

Blackie said casually to Jude, "I'll toss you to see who hits him. Five gets you five that I can knock him further than you can, Jude."

Jude Gordon didn't answer. He was looking at the stagehand, who was edging forward. The man bore a striking resemblance to his father.

It exploded something inside Jude's brain. He stepped forward and let go with all that was back of his wiry, powerful young body. He felt pain go through his knuckles as the man went down five feet away, rolled over on his face, and lay still. Blackie began to chuckle. He reached into his pocket and brought out five silver dollars.

"You win, Jude, I couldn't have knocked him that far—*Honey.*"

It was the singer. She had come up a short flight of steps that led down below the stage and now stood there, all golden in lights, and making Jude's heart do queer things.

She gave a cry and ran forward into Blackie's arms.

Blackie stood there, his arm around the singer's waist. "Come here, Jude, and meet the sweetest little girl on the prairie."

Jude went over, removing his hat as his mother had taught him to do. He stood there in front of the singer.

"Hello, Jude," Edwina greeted him, extending a slim hand. "You're all right. Say . . . you can take care of yourself. Blackie, he's handsome!"

"Cut it out," Blackie's voice said. "Jude's my pardner, not my rival. Find him another girl."

"I don't want another girl," Jude said, feeling his face flame.

"Come on down to the dressing room," Edwina said, leading the way down the steps. "It's beneath the stage. Follow me."

They went down.

CHAPTER TEN

EDWINA sat down at the dressing table, and Blackie relaxed on the couch. Jude sat stiffly on the edge of his chair, feeling ill at ease, listening to the bantering and endearments the two exchanged.

He was wondering how he could make a graceful bow out and get back to the hotel, but Edwina had a girl picked out for him.

She got up and went to the door, opened it, and disappeared into the hallway. Jude felt his stomach constrict. He wished at that moment that he were out of there and back on the farm. Blackie winked.

"Just stick around, Jude," he advised.

"I oughta go look up Tolson," Jude said. "He's shot through the hip and maybe. . . ."

Edwina came back through the doorway. With her was a dark young girl, very pretty, about Jude's age. She still wore her stage costume.

"This is Angelica," she said to them both. "She rooms with me upstairs," and then finished introductions.

"Hiya," Angelica said.

Blackie had raised upon one elbow. Jude wasn't blushing but something in his mien appeared to strike the two-gun rider as funny. He went off into laughter. "Come on, let's get out of here," he hooted. "Leave them alone."

Jude got up from the chair where he had been sitting. That constriction had hit his stomach again. "I guess I ought to get out and go back downtown," he said. "I sorta promised to look up Tolson," he finished weakly.

A knock, hard, short-rapping, and professional, came on the door.

It was the stagehand Jude had knocked down. He grinned a little and said, "Hello, cowpunch. Somebody here."

Nute Shelby pushed through the doorway. He was followed by Mike Kessler, the limping Joe, and Peanut, the day wrangler. Peanut stood rigidly, and in that moment he didn't look like a horse wrangler. There was dignity and a cool boredom in the way in which he slid his still square shoulders up against the wall beside the doorway.

He was an officer now.

They made an incongruous group.

Blackie was up off the couch now. He was looking at the trail boss. "Let's have it, Nute. How'd you find us here?"

"Made the rounds of the bars. Asked questions," was the curt reply.

"All right, you're here. Now what?"

"Tolson is dead. He bought himself some crutches when he got in town. I traced him from one bar to another. He was limping around and doing all right, but I wanted to be sure. Then he started across the tracks. Somebody got him there. In the back. His body is down at the undertaking parlor. Come on."

He went out. They followed down the hallway, Edwina with Blackie.

"Angelica and me will have to do a couple of more turns on

the stage and then we'll be through. We'll wait for you," she said.

They filed up the steps, across the now deserted stage with its drawn curtain, and down through the curtained doorway again. Somebody said laughingly, "These trail herd Texans don't waste any time, do they?"

The group of them stopped, bunched up, at the bar.

They drank and went out, led by Shelby, and clumped down the boardwalk. Their boots echoed hollowly in the night.

"What now?" Blackie asked Nute Shelby.

"Spread out and make the rounds of all the saloons. Drift in and see if you can see any NP punchers. Ask questions as to when they came in. They're drinking and talking. Some might boast and let a few words slip out."

"I've only seen five or six so far." Peanut's voice cut in. "Wheah you think the othuhs are?"

Nobody answered. They were cutting on down past more saloons now.

"The old man get in yet?" Blackie asked.

He and Nute were leading the others. "Yes," curtly, "on the late train. They're put up at the hotel."

He named it. It was the same hotel where Jude and Blackie had their room.

"The kid get in with them?"

"Yes."

Nute then stopped. The others in the little group stopped too. The trail boss said, "You're about all that's left sober out of the bunch. The others are over in the bawdy houses. Grady's around town somewhere. If you run into him tell him what to do. Meet me at the hotel in one hour."

"All right." Blackie speaking. "What did the old man say about that two hundred head?"

"Nothing. Got to expect things like that on a drive. We picked up a few strays on the way up. I insisted on an actual count. Twenty-eight hundred and forty-one head. Mike, you take this first place and spread out along the street. The rest of you the same. I'm going back to the hotel and wait."

Mike was slim and blond and about twenty-six. He stood beside Jude and eyed the inviting doors of the saloon. "And to think," he murmured, "that I might have become a scholar. But now I've got to go into a place where that vile stuff known as rotgut, red-eye, alcohol, and plain panther juice is

51

being sold to poor innocent cowpunchers. Tsk ... tsk ... tsk! Coming in for a drink, Jude?"

"I'll help you work the street," Jude answered.

He went in with Mike, who promptly headed for the bar. Jude left him there. He worked in and out of one saloon after another and finally found himself back on the main street. There was a kind of lean-to dive built alongside of a much larger building, and Jude went toward it. He didn't go in, but headed for a side window. He knew none of the NP outfit by sight, except the four who had been on the street that afternoon, but he cut around to the side and looked in a window.

At the bar, drinking with Harrison, was Grady.

Jude went in. He worked his way along until he came to a spot some ten feet away. He ordered a drink, hoping to listen. But the buck-toothed puncher had spotted him. He sneered, and Harrison turned slowly.

"Hello, farmer," Grady said contemptuously.

Jude said nothing.

"He's a nester that hooked himself onto the outfit to get a few square meals," Grady explained in a loud voice.

Harrison had turned slowly. His right hand was swollen and had a light bandage around it. But there was nothing wrong with the left one dropping down to his left hip.

"The bull whip kid, eh?" he grunted. "You made a mistake coming in here, younker. The worst mistake you ever made."

"I'm going to beat his head off," Grady sneered.

Harrison's hard voice cut in. "Hold it, Grady. I'll take care of this."

Jude had picked up his drink served by a wooden-faced bartender. He moved forward toward them. He was unarmed and he knew what was coming. And for some strange reason he felt no fear. It might have been the drinks. . . .

Harrison said, "Too bad you haven't got your bull whip with you, kid. This hand of mine won't be much good for another couple of weeks. And men don't do that kind of thing to Jim Harrison. It's out for you."

Then a voice came softly from back of them; a voice that Jude knew all too well. Blackie's.

"Not yet, Harrison!"

Harrison turned and froze. Grady's mouth was open. "You rat," Blackie said. "I don't mind a man stealing a few cows now and then. But a man don't turn coyote on his outfit.

Jude, he was going to take you. He can still do it, if you want. But Harrison is not going to use that good hand of his. It's up to you."

Jude pushed his farm-hardened young body away from the bar. Then he lunged.

CHAPTER ELEVEN

TEN MINUTES later they came out into the street. Blackie paused and looked back. He was still laughing. Grady was down on the floor, and Jim Harrison, head of the Nester Pool of cattle rustlers, had not moved. Jude wiped at the blood at his nose again, using a sleeve of the new shirt.

It had been quite a fight.

"By God, Jude, you surprise me more and more all the time," the older man said a little more seriously. "Grady outweighs you by a good twenty pounds, he's all muscle and no brain, and yet you took him. He knocked you down twice but you kept coming back for more, quick as a cat. If you could learn to use a gun as naturally as you use your fists, you'd be a young holy terror."

"I'll make out all right," Jude said. "He said he was going to lick me. I gave him his chance."

"He had his chance all right. So did Harrison. You notice how *he* stood fast and didn't make a move. I was hoping differently. He *knew* I was hoping differently. I was aching for him to make a move. Some day I'm going to kill that hombre and I wanted to do it tonight, but he wouldn't make a play. Come on, let's go across the street to the hotel."

The lobby was inviting and they went in. None of the others of the outfit had yet arrived. But there were three people with the trail boss.

Jude didn't have to look at the short, wiry man, the buxom woman sitting on the cowhide lounge beside him, and the impatiently pacing young woman in fashionable clothes to know that this was the T4 owner and his family.

"So that's what she looks like?" came Blackie's murmured

voice in Jude's ear. "She'd just left for the East when I joined the outfit."

"She's sure pretty," Jude observed.

"Yeah, and she sure knows it, too. But I want that. I'm going to have it."

Jude threw a side glance at his companion. There was something hard in Blackie's face; something that was almost brutal. Jude thought of Edwina the singer and said nothing.

Harry Travers was in his late forties, his leathery face showing the years he'd spent against the sun and under the stars. He'd probably fought in the Civil War too, Jude thought; like Peanut. He'd married his wife when she was seventeen. She hadn't been buxom then. She was now, though still in her thirties.

Introductions came first, Nute Shelby doing the honors. Nell Travers acknowledged them with a brief extension of a hand and a briefer nod, and resumed her restless pacing, something in her mien indicating that she was forgetting her heredity and remembering her environment of the past year or so.

"Anything to report?" grunted the foreman.

"Nothing on Tolson or the NP men," Blackie said, and then gave details of the fight across the street. "Grady was right there, drinking with Harrison, friendly as could be. Harrison's hand was bandaged where Jude cut it with the bull whip when he tried to draw on me, but there wasn't anything wrong with the other one. He wouldn't draw. It was the second chance today."

"You'd better put those guns away before you end up in trouble," Travers cut in in a drawling voice.

"Not while Harrison is packing his. That all, Nute?"

"That's all."

Blackie turned to Jude, who somehow had the idea that part of Blackie's conversation had been for the benefit of Nell Travers. She had picked up interest enough to stop her impatient pacing.

"In that case, I reckon we'll be going," the two-gun rider said. "Miss Travers, glad to have met you. See you later, boss."

Jude hesitated. "I think I'll go upstairs and—" he began, but Blackie's hand clasped him around the back of the neck and gave him a goodnatured shove.

"You're going upstairs, all right," he said softly in Jude's ear as they headed toward the street again. "But not here."

They entered the Prairie Dove again. It was still early. Blackie said, "Come on," and headed for a roulette table.

"Got those two silver dollars left, Jude?" he asked, grinning.

Jude brought them out.

"Then get on me. I'm steaming. We're going to roll."

He began to play the red and black and Jude, betting a dollar at a time, began to collect his winnings. Presently Blackie started to plunge. Jude followed him, taking in nine to one winnings. Sometimes they lost but usually they won. Blackie was plunging harder now. Once he bet ten dollars on the number thirteen and hit it on the nose. He looked sideways at Jude and grinned.

"You should have rode with me, Jude. I told you I can't lose."

They played on, and presently the dealer began to get worried. Jude was three hundred and forty dollars to the good and Blackie must have had close to eighteen hundred. They were using chips now. Five-dollar chips. The dealer glanced over his shoulder. Jude saw him nod to a man who came threading through, shouldering his way past players.

"I'll take over," he announced.

Blackie paused, leaning over a pile of chips.

"Yeah?" he said, his eyes narrowing.

"What's wrong with the other dealer?" Jude asked.

The new man shrugged. He was hard-faced, hard-eyed, and there was a bulge in the right sleeve of his white shirt. A hidden derringer.

"Dealers have to be relieved," he said curtly. "One hour on, thirty minutes off to sit down."

"We haven't been playing an hour."

"House rules, cowboy. Take it or leave it."

"I'm leaving it," Blackie said.

The dealer spun the wheel and then spun the ball in its groove, in the opposite direction. Blackie had put one hundred dollars on the black. Jude, something warning him, didn't bet. The dealer had his hands on the table now, fingers beneath the edge. The white ball dropped into the red. Blackie bet on the black once more and once more it was red. One hundred dollars a throw. Four more players were with them, betting from one to five dollars. Jude wasn't long in realizing that it now was a game between the dealer and Blackie. He let his chips lie where they were stacked.

Then Blackie made a four-hundred dollar bet on the red. The dealer leaned forward over the table, hands resting on the edge of it, fingers out of sight below.

Right at that moment two things happened almost simultaneously. Blackie did a dive to the floor and looked beneath the table; and the dealer jerked back his right hand, slapping a .41 derringer into the palm.

Blackie had merely gone down on one knee and Jude's yell of warning caught him.

A gun roared. It roared twice more. Blackie, half up across the table, held the smoking gun in his right hand as the crooked dealer went down on his back, shot three times through the chest. Bedlam broke loose. Men yelled and dived for cover. Others stood frozen, too startled to move. Blackie straightened and, still gripping the pistol in his right hand, went around back of the table as the two deputy marshals came plowing their way through the crowd.

Blackie stood astraddle of the dead dealer's body. His other gun was out now, and his black eyes were blazing.

"Hand over those guns, cowpunch," ordered one of the marshals, advancing. "You can't get away with that in here. This is Abilene."

"This is Texas, mister. I can get away with it. He drew on me with a sleeve gun. It's here on the floor. And come around here and take a look at these fancy little gadgets under the edge of this table. Nice bunch of skunks."

One of the other players had gone down beneath the table. He came up, fighting to get to his feet in the close packed crowd.

"Men," he called out loudly, "this wheel's crooked. I call on you to witness it. They played the law of averages until these cowmen began to win. Then they slipped in a crooked dealer to get back their lost cash. This finishes the Prairie Dove. It's a crooked layout!"

The marshals, a little less belligerent now, came gingerly forward. They went beneath the table and looked. They came up. They looked at the dead man on the floor, saw the .41 derringer, and heard the rumbling mutter of the crowd. One of the men looked at Blackie.

"All right, cowpunch. Self-defense. I wish Hickock was here."

Blackie said, "Pick up your chips, Jude, and let's cash 'em in. I'm taking a few hundred from this dealer's rack to make up for those last bets. Come on."

They shouldered through a path respectfully opened for them and went across to the wall opposite the bar. Back of a wire cage, was a slender man wearing a green eyeshade and black "garters" on his shirt sleeves above the elbows.

Blackie shoved his hat over the counter, turning it upside down. A stream of chips cascaded out. One rolled off the counter and struck the floor.

"Pay off," he ordered.

The dealer reached out with slender fingers and separated the chips into different-colored piles. He rifled the stacks expertly, said, "Eighteen hundred and fifty," and reached below the counter. Blackie said, "Nineteen hundred and fifty," and reached through to grasp the dealer's wrist.

Somebody said, "This means the end of the Prairie Dove. Too bad."

"Too bad, hell!" replied another's voice. "Any house can win on percentages. Any time they won't let a man with a lucky streak take out a few dollars they ought to go out of business. Serves 'em right!"

Blackie had let go of the dealer's wrist. Jude turned. He saw Harrison and he saw Grady. And he saw Harrison's left hand going to the pistol. Then Jude's actions became automatic. Some strange impulse caused him to reach for the pistol at Blackie's left hip. It came free easily from the worn holster. He spun with it in his hand as Harrison's gun roared.

Jude didn't know how to shoot from the hip. This much he had learned from firing the old Sharps. A man trying to hit a target didn't shoot that way. He took careful aim.

Jude lined the sights of the heavy revolver straight at Harrison's belly and pulled the trigger, remembering what Blackie had told him.

The gun roared. The barrel kicked up because he had been holding it too loosely. He was unaware of Blackie wheeling, the other gun out, staring. Harrison was going down in a lazy sort of way. The heavy bullet, catching him in the throat, had flung him back against the bar by the sheer power of its shock, and the head of the NP rustler pool was half falling, half sliding as he went down. His bandaged right hand made a kind of thudding sound against the brass rail of the bar.

He was dead. Grady made a dash toward the front door.

Blackie's quiet calm voice said, "Jude, you saved my life. I won't forget. Cash in your chips while I watch the crowd."

There wasn't any reason to watch the crowd. A man said loudly that it was self-defense and that the other man had fired the first shot. The two disgruntled marshals were quick too. They agreed. Jude cashed in his chips, sliding the money into his pocket. He was sick, his stomach all upset. He hadn't meant to kill a man.

"My God!" an awed voice said. "Did you see that kid move? Like a streak of lightning. I've seen four men killed in Abilene, including one shot by Hickock, but I never saw anything to match it."

Jude started pushing his way through the crowd.

CHAPTER TWELVE

JUDE GOT UP early the next morning and went down to breakfast. He went into the big hotel dining room and sat down at a corner table, conscious that men were staring at him. Nute Shelby was eating breakfast with the Travers family. Jude saw the girl Nell looking at him. He couldn't tell whether it was through curiosity or because of the fact that he'd killed the head of the Nester Pool the night before in a gunfight. The buzz of conversation that had ceased at his entrance soon resumed. Jude ordered and ate.

Shelby pushed back from the table and came over. He sat down and rolled a cigarette.

"Mornin'," he said curtly.

"Morning," Jude said.

The girl brought his coffee and he finished the meal.

"Where's Blackie?" the foreman asked.

"At the Prairie Dove, I reckon."

Shelby's eyebrows raised. "Don't you know?"

"No, I reckon I don't. I didn't stay there last night."

"I see. Got all your stuff bought?"

"I got to get a bedroll, shaving outfit, saddle and a pair of chaps."

"I'll go with you to pick the saddle. I know what you need for work down there. When you start pulling a bogged down cow out of a mudhole you want something that won't come apart. Got enough money?"

"I got plenty."

"Then let's get going." the foreman said, rising. He was packing his gun. He looked at Jude. "Where's your six-shooter?"

Jude told him. A harsh look came over Shelby's face. "Go back upstairs and get it! I was around town late last night trying to round up the boys after that fight. More NP men are reported in town and they've sworn to get you."

So that was why the foreman was going with him to buy a saddle. They went out into the street. It was teeming with the usual early morning traffic. Jude felt strange with the .44 revolver stuck down the front of his waistband. He made his purchases under Shelby's critical eye, including eight hundred rounds of cartridges. He got the blacksnake with the new popper and the spares. By the time he finished the hotel room was becoming crowded with equipment. Shelby had gone up with him. There was a new respect in the trail boss's eyes. Jude was no longer a nester kid. He was one of the outfit now, and again he'd done them a good turn. He'd killed the man everybody knew but couldn't prove was head of the rustler ring.

Shelby picked up Jude's new belt and broke out a box of cartridges. He filled it while Jude stacked his purchases. When they went out into the street again the lead-studded belt encircled Jude's wiry waist; it and the six-shooter felt as if they weighed a ton.

"We're going to hunt up the boys and get out of here," Shelby said. "Travers' orders. The NP men are out to get us after that fracas last night. They're spoiling for a pitched battle."

"I'm sorta sorry about that."

"Don't be," snapped the foreman. "Blackie would have got him anyhow before we left town. It was in the cards, and you did us a good turn. Soon as we find the boys and I get somebody to side you, I'll go to the jail and get Bugger out. Dirty trick, putting that man in jail. He's a good hand."

"Grady's across the street," Jude replied, pointing to the lean-to gambling place and bar where the fight had taken place. Back of it was a shabby-looking hotel.

"Grady won't be going back with us," came the grunted

answer. "I'm firing him the minute I set eyes on him. He always was a little too friendly with Harrison."

Jude asked about the lost cattle. Shelby shook his head. They were heading across the tracks toward the bawdy houses. "I've got a man at the stockyards but they didn't show up. Going back we'll spread out a few miles apart and check any herd coming up." And he went on ahead to describe the markers.

"But we're rolling out of here the minute the outfit gets together," Shelby added.

They found Mike in one of the bars. He had been up all night and was happily, gloriously drunk.

"Come on," ordered the foreman curtly.

"I'd rather sing." He rocked back on his heels and grabbed at the bar.

"Get hold of his other arm, Jude," Shelby grunted. "Come on, Mike."

"But I like this place," Mike Kessler protested as they made a threesome toward the front door. They rocked out into the street.

Four men passed them. One was a burly individual with a fat, sour visage above a big belly. His eyelashes were gone. The lids were red-rimmed. He gave them a challenging look, made a remark under his breath to his companions.

"Tolliver," Shelby told Jude. "Red Tolliver. Close friend of Harrison and a mean man in a fight. Don't forget his face."

"Be pretty hard to forget it."

"Don't forget mine either," Mike mumbled happily.

Cic came by on the boardwalk. He was in pretty good shape.

"Mawnin', boys," he greeted them, and looked at Jude. "I been hearin' reports about you, boy. Good work."

"Cic, we're getting out of here right away to avoid trouble," Shelby told the older man. "Start rounding up the boys. You go with Jude over to the Prairie Dove to get Blackie. And keep your hand close to your gun. The NP are after his scalp for downing Harrison last night, and I just passed Red Tolliver and three others going that way. Keep out of their way."

"Me and trouble are old friends, boss."

"You heard what I said!" snapped the foreman, his eyes blazing. "Keep *out* of trouble. Now get going. Seen Pokey?"

"Nobody has. He just plumb disappeared within an hour after we got in last evenin'."

Shelby went on down the street (as Jude later found out, he went to the undertaking parlor to pay for Tolson's coffin and other burial expenses) and the two others went in the opposite direction.

"I sure been hearing plenty of talk this mornin' about you, Jude," Cic remarked, reaching for his tobacco sack. "Everybody's talkin' about how that kid cowpuncher plumb salivated Harrison. Wouldn't have meant too much if Harrison hadn't been packin' two guns and shot first."

"I'm no cowpuncher," Jude said.

"You will be," he said succinctly.

The front door of the Prairie Dove was padlocked . . . about the only saloon in town that was. They rounded the corner and went down the side street to the back, into an alley. A flight of stairs ran up to a landing that made entrance to the hall on the second floor. They clumped up and entered. All over the place was the smell of cheap perfume.

"Question is," Cic said, scratching his head with an index finger, "now where's the domain of our romantic Blackie and his bee-utiful bride of a night."

"I don't know." Jude grinned uncertainly.

"Well, boy, I know how to find out. You stand by and catch me as they throw me out."

They tried a few doors with varying results. Cic finally stuck his head cautiously through a door leading to a corner room. He turned, grinning. "We struck paydirt this time, boy. Come on."

Jude gingerly followed him into a large, well furnished room with a big bed in one corner. Blackie was in bed in it.

"You better get rolling," Cic advised. "We're hauling out today."

Blackie's grunt came plainly. "We spend weeks driving up the trail just to have a little fun, and now after one night the boss says to go back. You tell him I said go to hell. I've got seventeen hundred dollars left and I'm going to spend part of it right here. If the outfit is getting out of town to avoid trouble, then they don't need me. If it's just a matter of hitching up and hauling out, then they don't need me for that either. You tell Nute I said to go on without me. I've got some business that'll take me a few days. Tell him I'll show up in time. Jude, you put my saddle and stuff in the hotel room we had. Take the bedroll on the back to the ranch. Don't leave me a horse. I'll take a stage and beat you home."

He slid back under the covers and smoked, stretched out. His two guns hung on the head of the bedstead.

CHAPTER THIRTEEN

THE TRAVERS family was having supper in the T4 ranchhouse. The owner himself sat at the head of the table, his wife to his right and his daughter to his left. "Colonel" Sutherworth ate at the opposite end.

To the men of the outfit he was "Peanut" the wrangler. In the house he was Colonel Sutherworth, a secret rigidly kept by the members of the family and Jessie, the colored cook. Two meals of the day he ate with the men, but in the evening the former Confederate officer dined with the family in the house.

Jessie came in with a big steaming bowl in her dark hands. She began to serve, and a touch of annoyance twisted the corners of Nell Travers' pretty mouth.

"Jessie," she said tightly, "How many times have I told you since we arrived home that you serve from the *left* side?"

"Yassum," agreed Jessie, and shifted position. She was still slightly confused by the new turn of events. Before "Miss Nell" had gone away for a year of schooling back East, the meals had simply been put on the table like the cook did down in the dugout. And now. . . .

Jessie served.

Travers looked over at his petulant daughter and then at his wife. Amusement was in his eyes.

Jessie went back to the kitchen through a curtained doorway. Bugger, who customarily ate with her, was busy over his plate.

"I jes' don't understand that Miss Nell no mo'," the woman complained.

Bugger guffawed. "You'all jes' don't savvy, woman," he grinned. "You-all oughta been back in Gawgia when my mammy an' pappy worked fuh the cunnel's folks. My mammy was a cook an' my pappy was the butler. Mos' nigguhs worked in the fields an' you had to be somebody real 'special to be a butler. Dinin' tables a hunned foot long an' enough silvuh plates an' stuff to load down a wagon. You's jus' ignorant, thass all."

"All right, then you-all go in and serve 'em," snapped back the harassed Jessie, "since you know it all."

She started a return trip to the dining room and Bugger's guffaws of derision followed her.

In the dining room they finally finished the meal. The girl had gone to the front room, taken something from her father's desk, and returned. She came back and unrolled some paper on the table, pushing aside the dishes. Mrs. Travers looked dubious but the girl's father obviously was interested. The tide was turning. That trail herd to Abilene had brought in more money than he had suspected could be made in a year.

Travers bent over the plans for the new house. He looked at his daughter and chuckled fondly.

"So that's where so much of the money I couldn't spare to send you went?" he asked. "I had to borrow from the bank in Alden, and talk my head off to get it. And all the time you were spending it on one of them fancy—"

"Those, Father. Not them."

" 'Those, Father,' " he mimicked. "You were spending it on one of those fancy architects to draw up plans for a fancy house. Well, let's have a look at 'em."

He took the papers, peering this way and that, a frown wrinkling his brow.

"I'm damned if I can make head or tails of it," he finally said. He raised his face and looked at the man at the other end of the table. "Come here, Colonel. You know anything about this business?"

"As a mattuh of fact, Sergeant, ah had some of this in college. Let's see."

"You mean you savvy all these fancy lines an' drawings?"

"Why, suttinly. It's a nice-looking house. A low front veranda moah suited to the west—"

"Porch. Where the hell's the porch? I'm damned if I can see it."

The former colonel pulled up a chair and began to explain. Travers listened, watched, and a light of excitement came into the owner's eyes. He finally rose, pushing back his chair.

"All right," he said with his decisive way of speaking. "We'll build it. A hundred yards north of here, where the ground rises a bit higher."

"And a little farther away from the other buildings," his daughter put in.

"We'll get at it in the morning, freight our supplies from town. Colonel, I always wanted you to have a better job than wrangling, but you insisted because you said it was easier than regular punching. Tomorrow you take charge of the building. Get workmen out here. Use any of the hands you want. But we start building tomorrow. Jessie!" he called.

Jessie stuck her head through the curtains. She wore a maid's cap and a frilled white apron now, as of the last four days. Things were changing on the T4.

"Yessuh?"

"Tell Bugger to go get that young nester kid Jude and bring him in here."

"Yassuh." Her head disappeared, and presently the kitchen door rattled.

"Jude?" Sutherworth asked.

"That nester Nute picked up in Kansas. He's a team man. He'll do the freightin'."

"Isn't that the boy who shot Jim Harrison in Abilene?" Mrs. Travers inquired.

It was the wrangler who answered. "Yes, ma'am, that's the boy. Only he's not a boy. He's eighteen, he's got a little moah education than most of these heah cowpunchers, and he's the quickest man to learn I evah saw."

Nell Travers sniffed. "I suppose he thinks that because he shot the head rustler of the Nester Pool he'll be too good to handle a freight team to build a new house. It will do him good to stay where he belongs—behind a team. And if he's got any ideas that because he's being called up here to the house—"

Her father shot her a look, a glint in his eye. "If you're worried about him moonin' around you because I own the outfit, I don't think it'll cause you any trouble. I watched that kid all the way down the line. One thing I'll say for Nute —he knows how to pick men. That kid tends to his own business, he keeps his eyes and ears open and learns things, and if he don't get too handy with that gun he already can handle so fast, he'll make one of the best hands this outfit ever had. Nute likes him, and that's good enough for me. You're getting too big for your britches, young lady."

"Father!"

"Call me Pa, dammit!" he roared.

CHAPTER FOURTEEN

JUDE KNOCKED and then opened the door and entered.

"Come in, Jude," Travers called.

Jude went over to where the two men were working over the plans. He nodded to Mrs. Travers. "How are you, Ma'am?"

The girl he nodded at, but did not speak to her. She was a lovely thing, with her russet-colored hair and blue eyes, but he had sensed in her impatient pacing in the hotel in Abilene, in her refusal to come home with the outfit, that she was spoiled to the point of arrogance. He was taking a more decided dislike to her every time he saw her.

The ranchman twisted around in his chair. "Jude, these plans are for a new house we're going to build over there a hundred yards from here."

"Two hundred, Father," his daughter put in. "I want to choose the location myself."

Her father ignored that. He said to Jude. "So, son, tomorrow morning I want you and Pokey to hitch up the chuckwagon and go to Alden. I'll meet you in town. I'm going to buy two new freight wagons and start hauling supplies right away. Col.—Peanut here is going to be in charge of the building. You'll be in charge of the freighters. Peanut will tell you what to buy. What we can't get in town we'll order."

"All right," Jude answered. "Anything else?"

"That's all for the present. If you and the other freighter can get a couple of good helpers—and I'll fire any man who won't work—you ought to be able to make one round trip a day. I want you to make it, come hell or high water. We'll have a fall roundup on our hands pretty soon and I'll need every puncher I can get hold of."

"All right," Jude said.

The girl's eyes were glinting. "Mr. Gordon," she said icily, "it would be a little more mark of respect to address the owner as 'sir' or 'Mr. Travers.' And, while we're on the subject, you'll address me as 'Miss Travers'."

"I'm not aiming to address you at all. I'm just aiming to keep out of your way," was the quiet reply.

Travers exploded in a roar of laughter. "Haw-haw-haw!" he bellowed. "That's one time you got what was comin' to you, 'Miss Travers.' You stick around this ranch long enough young lady, and we'll soon get yore head out of the clouds and down where it belongs. All right, Jude, you tell Pokey —and you keep him sober in town tomorrow."

The T4 came alive before daybreak the next morning. Shelby seemed to be everywhere, handing out orders for the day. Travers showed up as Jude came out of the corral with two bridled horses and began harnessing.

"Peanut made up a list of what we'll need first, Jude," he said. "Mostly mortar for the foundation. We'll haul the rock from the foot of Bald Knob. I'm going in town in the buggy to see about some more men and I'll run into you there. Get loaded as soon as you can and keep Pokey out of the saloons."

Jude nodded, fastening on horse collars. He finished the four, found out where the storehouse was, and unloaded. By the time he finished and hauled up before the dugout door Pokey was ready. They removed the tarps and staves that covered the bed and rattled off down past the ranchhouse. The road angled north and west, dropping in a gentle incline across the flat to a big wash half a mile below. Wheels crunched into damp ruts as they worked across.

Alden came in sight, some fourteen miles from the ranch. Its scattered buildings were sprawled on a gently sloping knoll, bare of trees. It was a much larger place than Jude had imagined. Being the only town within sixty miles, it drew trade from every rancher and nester in the country.

Harness rattled behind the plodding team and Jude looked back. Travers swerved around them behind a span of trotting blacks, his daughter beside him. Jude tipped his hat, ignoring the cold look she gave him. The buggy grew smaller on the rutted road ahead. Pokey spat over the front wheel and wiped his "splay puss" mustache.

"She used to be a nice younker around the ranch. Regular

66

tomboy, all over the place. Ride like a man and a dinger at ropin' a calf. But not any more. Too many hifalutin' idees she got in thet fancy school they sent her to. But I reckon she'll git back, give her time."

"I don't like her," Jude said. "All I want to do is keep out of her way."

Pokey cackled. "Then you're sure different from most of these other cow hands. They go outa their way to get a chance to tip their hats an' say, 'Howdy, ma'am.' Little good it'll do 'em. Bet you a bottle of whiskey thet when we get that big house finished she'll be givin' parties an' hirin' maids an' servin' tea." He wrinkled up his nose at the last thought. "Well, I guess Travers can afford it now. He can easy put three thousand up the trail to Abilene every year. Few more years of that an' he'll be worth a million."

He changed the subject, pointing toward a jumble of red sandstone in the square. "See thet? It's a new courthouse goin' up. Two story an' even a cupola. People got together last year an' voted ninety thousand dollars fer it an' the new jail. We elected our first sheriff last year. Jim Underhill. Good man. Yep, we're comin' up in the world."

They were entering town and Jude didn't answer. He was staring at a man and woman who stood on the porch of the general store and stage station, waiting for their luggage to be tossed down.

Blackie had come back and he had brought Edwina with him.

CHAPTER FIFTEEN

POKEY CRACKED the four into a trot. They rattled westward along what soon would be the south side of the square, past the workmen toiling away at the red sandstones. Pokey cut to the right past the hotel and came up in back of the store, where a giant wagon yard sprawled over three acres of land, surrounded by a high fence. Inside the fence were new wagons and buggies of every description, and a lot of farm implements bought for the nesters but which appeared to have been sitting there in the sun and rain for quite some time.

"Whoa, blast you. Whoa!" Pokey bawled, and hauled up hard on the four lines directly at the double back doors of the store. The hub wheels hit hard against the loading platform and Pokey wrapped the lines around the set brake handle. He displayed remarkable agility in going over to the hub-high platform and turned as Jude followed.

"I saw the old man's buggy out front of the store," he said with the manner of a conspirator. "He is in there talkin' to Sol Martin. Any time the local gamblers get hit hard they come to Sol. I've seen him hand out four thousand in gold with no note signed. An' when they bring it back he won't take any interest. As long as he's got stuff on the shelves, people who ain't got money can get it on credit. He don't lose any either—not even from them cowthievin' nesters. But never mind that. You can see the old man in there. Now, Jude, right next door is the back end of a saloon, an' you an' me can sorta slip in there an' pick up a drink an' get a quart."

"I'll get the quart," Jude cut in. "I'll hide it under the seat and it'll stay there until we get out of town."

"But that'll at least be two or three hours," Pokey wailed.

"I know. But the old man said no saloons, Pokey," Jude smiled, and clapped him on the shoulder.

Pokey went snorting into the back of the store and Jude dropped down the four steps at the end of the loading platform. He opened the rear door of the saloon and went in, had a drink, paid for the quart, and came back the same way. He disposed of the liquor, grinning a little as he hid it beneath the loading platform. Then he went inside.

Sol and Travers were sitting inside, the merchant going over his account books.

"I got it at eight thousand, seven hundred forty-one dollars and eighty-six cents, Harry," Jude heard Sol say. "Does that check with your figures?"

"You know dam' well, Sol, that I never keep any figures," the T4 owner replied. "Entirely too much trouble, except in a tally book, yourn are good enough for me."

"That includes the six hundred cash you wanted for Nellie," Sol added, and Jude forced down a grin. She might be "hifalutin'" now, but a lot of her schooling had come from money borrowed from Sol Martin's big safe.

"That include the interest on the loan?" Travers asked.

"I'm a merchant, not a money lender, Harry. If I've got it, you boys can get it. There have been times when I had to send my son with signed notes to pay for what my string of freighters brought back, but somehow we've all managed to pull through. And now there's this new railroad in Abilene, with the East crying for Texas beef. I see good times ahead.

"So do I. Lordy, the prices they ain't paying in Abilene. Nute said three groups of buyers came loping out to start bidding against each other."

The merchant leaned back in his chair and pushed the square, old-fashioned spectacles up into his shock of hair. He nodded, similing genially.

"That's what makes good business, Harry. The bidding."

"That's why I want to do some more before the bidding starts, Sol. This new house is costing plenty, but I'll still have some left. I might need more."

"So?"

"Henson and his wife want to sell out over on Duck Creek. He told me so before I left with the herd. My north boundary meets his south boundary, and we've never found it necessary to keep any line riders between us. When my boys see any of his stuff they throw it back north. His do the same with my T4 brand. He's running about a thousand head now, but says his wife an' him are getting old and want to get out. Claims it's too late for him to start driving up the trail to Kansas. He's cattle poor and the damned nesters are stealing him dry. I can get the outfit pretty cheap. I might need some more cash."

Jude pretended to be examining a group of bridles hanging from a rack, the raw, yellow leather feeling good to his touch.

"You can get it if you need it," Sol Martin said. "Buy and I'll back you all I can."

Travers started to reply but Jude didn't hear the answer. For at that moment a pair of soft hands slid around from behind and covered his eyes and he felt the imprint of a kiss on his cheek. He turned.

Edwina took his cheeks between her hands and kissed him squarely on the lips.

"Jude!" she exlcaimed delightedly. "You gun-throwing cowboy!"

Blackie came forward, grinning, hand extended. They shook.

"Hello, Jude," Blackie grinned. "We finally got here. Rode all night on the stage to make the last lap. How's things?"

"All right, I guess. We got back fine. No trouble except the usual amount of rain and wind. How's Angelica?"

Edwina laughed and so did Blackie. He was wearing a new suit, but the two heavy pistols showed their bulge beneath the coat.

"She sends her regards and threatens to follow us out here," Edwina smiled. "I think you kind of took her heart away from her, Jude. Shame on you, you handsome cowboy."

A man strolled by casually, toward the back door, and Jude said to Edwina, "Excuse me."

He went out the back door. Pokey was fumbling frantically beneath the wagon seat. He turned, his face growing red.

"I—uh—think I lost my jackknife," he mumbled. "Some of the boys is whittlin' out on the front porch an' I sorta couldn't find it."

"Take mine." Jude brought out the new one he'd bought in Abilene. "It's razor sharp."

Pokey glared, slammed the knife into his pocket, and stalked indignantly back into the store, head held high. Jude followed him inside.

Travers came out, after settling up with Sol Martin, and they got busy loading the wagon with two new tents for the extra men, plus the other things Peanut had required. Travers disappeared, ostensibly to hunt up some men. Two of Sol's help hooked onto the two huge new freight wagons and rolled them up near the big gate and began greasing the axles. They stood high off the ground with broad iron tires.

"We'll need 'em," the sweating Pokey grunted, heaving at a sack. "Just you wait until we get caught in a downpour. Them wheels'll go clean to the hubs. I know. You got your job cut out fer you, Jude."

Noon came. They broke off long enough to eat. By that time two teams of four each, bought from the livery and complete with harness, had been hooked to the two wagons and had disappeared in the direction of the lumber yard. At one o'clock the loading was done. Jude wiped the sweat from his face and straightened. He removed the grain nose bags from the horses' heads, bent and retrieved the bottle beneath the loading platform, and got ready to crawl up for the return trip.

Then Blackie and a big bluff man of about fifty came

70

through the rear door. The man looked like any ordinary cowman except for the star on his shirt front. Jim Underhill, the first sheriff.

They shook hands at Blackie's introduction, and Underhill's penetrating but good-natured eyes took in Jude, the pistol at his right hip. "So you got Harrison in Abilene?" he commented. "Blackie told me all about it, son. Long as you wait for the other man to shoot first, you won't have any trouble with me."

"I don't expect any trouble," Jude said. "But if it comes I reckon I'll have to judge accordingly."

He looked at Blackie. "You coming back to the ranch?"

Blackie grinned, shaking his head. "Jim's just offered me a job as deputy sheriff, Jude."

"Taking it?" low-voiced.

"You bet I'm taking it. No more getting a shirt torn off by a steer's horn going down in a stampede for Blackie. I'm through with the cow business, Jude. But I'll be out to get my stuff."

Jude put down his disappointment, hiding it beneath a poker face. He said, "Sounds like a good job. I wish you luck."

And in that moment he knew that his and Blackie's trails had parted. They would see each other at intervals and still be friends. But Blackie was a lawman now and, too, there was Edwina. He wondered if they were married.

Jude stuck out his hand again. "Well, I guess we'd better get going. I'll run into you now and then, I guess."

"Yup, we better get goin'," Pokey put in, his eyes instinctively glancing back of the seat. He crawled up and unwrapped the lines. Blackie stepped forward.

"One word of warning, Jude. The NP outfit with Red Tolliver leading left Abilene the day before Edwina and me took the stage. They'll be in in a few days. Watch your horizons, boy."

CHAPTER SIXTEEN

THE T4—the T was for Travers and the 4 for the four years he had spent in the Civil War—became more of a construction camp than a ranch in the weeks that followed. Fifteen workmen were housed in the two new tents and under Peanut's crisp supervision the big foundation of red sandstone took shape in what looked like irregular squares and the walls began to rise. Jude worked from daylight until dark, making daily trips to Alden, loading and unloading, loading and unloading. . . . His life seemed to be made up of nothing else. He ate hungrily at all times and his body, which had been hard enough, took on weight even while it became lean and tough. He saw Blackie nearly every day, wearing the badge of a deputy sheriff. And from all reports Blackie was making a good one.

He and Edwina were not openly living together. They shared separate rooms in the two-story hotel on the northeast corner of the square. The north side itself housed a line of gambling places and saloons and two restaurants. Jude wore his gun all the time, for Red Tolliver was back and Red was openly boasting. In the store silent, surly-looking nesters—men who wore plowmen's shoes while in town and then later shifted to riding boots—stared hard at him and gave him a wide berth. Jude went his way, wary, quiet, and never turning his back on a man. Reports drifted in that Blackie had laid down the law to Tolliver. And Blackie was a bad man to deal with. Jude heard other reports that Edwina was going to open up a place, a general gambling hall and saloon, where she would sing. The town was growing; the second story of the courthouse was now up and the roof going on. Men were drifting in. You could hear all sorts of rumors: that the cowmen over a hundred-mile radius were hiring "exterminators" to take care of rustling nesters: that the nesters were hiring killers to take care of the big owners.

Jude went his way and the building supplies piled higher

and higher beside the newly erected structure until there came a day when Peanut said they had about enough.

"Any more we need can be taken care of without too much trouble, ah reckon, Jude," he said that late afternoon as Jude and his helper finished unloading. "We're startin' the fall roundup next week anyhow an' you'll be needed."

Jude nodded at the little man and watched the helper lead the teams away. He reached up into the big wagon and brought down his .44-40 repeater from the wagon seat.

Peanut's eyes nodded approval. "You shuh got a level head on you, son," he said. "Just because ah'm a buildin' man now is no reason why ah don't hear things. The Nester Pool is out to get you, son. Harrison was theah best bet. You eliminated him. They won't fo-get. Keep yo' eyes open, son."

"I'm depending on Blackie, Colonel," Jude smiled, for he and Peanut now were on familiar terms. "I don't want any trouble with anybody. I just don't want to get caught on the short end, that's all."

The other man's stern face relaxed in a smile. "Don't worry, son. You won't. Ah know men."

And that, coming from a man who had been through four years of shot and shell, was something to warm Jude's young heart.

They rolled out early the next morning, as usual, and Jude, wearing his chaps, went beneath the saddle shed and brought out his riding gear, carrying it toward the horse corral. Bugger had just driven them in, swinging down to put the pole gate into place. Jude watched the other riders catch their mounts, holding back because he was unfamiliar with corral procedure. He might get a horse that belonged to another man. When the riders thinned out he took his rope and went in, selecting a blocky-looking sorrel with four white feet. The animal was what was known as a "cream sorrel," and it was built for work; a deep barrel, a short body, and sturdy legs.

Mike Kessler, already mounted and awaiting Nute Shelby's orders for the day, looked over at Cic and grinned. Cic said significantly, "Just stand by an' see he don't get hurt."

"Slim" Connors, the bronk stomper of the outfit, twisted his swivel hips up into the saddle and said, "Thet sorrel's a good hoss but hard to handle."

"Let the kid alone," Cic cut in sharply.

"He's got to learn all by himself," Mike said. "But don't

73

worry—Jude can take care of himself. You boys just help me stand by to haze in case Jude gets into trouble."

The cream sorrel with the four white feet was cagey. Jude eyed another horse, went in with his loop swinging, then spun and caught the ducking sorrel. He drew it up to short length along the rope and put on the bridle, forcing its clenched teeth apart. It stood, quivering, wary. It sidled a bit as the blanket and then the saddle struck its sleek back. Jude cinched up tight, removed the rope from its neck, coiled it, fastened it on the saddle, and took up the reins.

Bugger stood by the corral gate, grinning a white-toothed grin. He knew every horse in the cavvy as well as he knew Jessie. He knew that cream sorrel. Bugger got his hand on the gate, all ready to "turn 'im out."

Jude grasped the reins in his left hand and then the left side of the head stall too. He pulled the sorrel's head around hard as his foot found the stirrup and he mounted. He straightened and let go of the head stall. Then something exploded beneath him and he felt himself sailing through the air. He landed on his left side and rolled over twice.

He got up, grim-lipped, and dusted himself off, thankful that he had hit on his left side. A number of men, wearing pistols, had had hips broken by falling on their guns.

Jude strode toward the sorrel. It stood across the corral, facing him, ears pointed and nostrils flaring. He was aware that Cic, Slim, and Mike were watching. So was Nute Shelby.

"Open that gate, Bugger," Jude called over his shoulder.

He took up the trailing reins and got ready to swing up a second time. The cream sorrel was half crouched, waiting. This time, when Jude hit leather, he hooked his rowels into the cinch to hang on. The sorrel went into action, straight toward the open gate.

"Ride 'im, Jude, ride 'im!" yelled Bugger.

The sorrel went out into the open, bucking at every jump, twisting his blocky body from side to side, his head down between his legs. He headed straight for the ranchhouse and, right in front of the east porch, went up sunfishing and came down twisting.

He came down alone. Jude struck heavily, almost on his face, and three riders came spurring by hard to haze the sorrel. Cic plunged in, rowelling his horse hard, and grabbed the dangling reins. He came leading the animal back as Jude got up and dusted himself off for the second time. He became aware then that Travers, his wife, and his daughter were standing on the porch in the morning dawn. The T4 owner still had a breakfast fork in one hand.

Jude found himself looking straight into Nell Travers' triumphant eyes.

"A freighter, you said you were," she laughed softly. "I never thought cowboys told the truth, but I apologize, Mr. Gordon. You told the truth. You're a freighter. You better take off those chaps and go back to hauling lumber."

Travers was more sympathetic. "A horse is easy to handle, son, once he knows who's boss. You just happened to pick a mean one. Nute should have known better."

"He's not mean," Jude said.

He mounted a third time, right in front of the porch, his face grim with determination. This time he held back on the reins enough to make the sorrel hold up its head a bit, not getting the bit between its teeth. They tore up the ground, the sorrel pitching in a circle until the animal, almost crashing into the side of the dining dugout, finally gave it up. It knew who was boss. Jude reined it over toward the corrals where a silent Nute Shelby had witnessed the whole show.

Jude said to Nute, quite casually, "Where you want me to work today?"

"Take the south boundary over near Double Mountain River. Better get some grub from the cook house. Cic'll go with you. Work everything back this direction. Better to start combing the brakes now than at roundup time. Push 'em all back."

They went south in the early morning sun, the two of them side by side.

"There's old Double Mountain," Cic said. "She don't look much now, but you oughta see her when we get a heavy rain. She comes bustin' down hell bent for election, all muddy and mad, takin' everything hard that gets in her way. That's when some of these damned dirty nesters get in their worst work. They drive a dozen cows with calves right down to the edge of the water and then down the cows with rifles. They float downstream for miles before the water goes down; an' by thet time the thieves have driven the bawlin' calves onto their own places, gotched and branded. We know it's T4 stuff but we ain't got any way of provin' it."

"Suppose you caught one rebranding or shooting?"

"Bring him in alive, if you can. If you can't, bring him in

dead. That's why Blackie bought that gun for you. But Jim Underhill is square, and if you can prove a clear case of rustlin', there won't be any trouble with the law. Underhill knows what we're up ag'in'. He ain't taking any sides. After all, Travers don't own his ranges any more than the rest of the cattlemen in Texas. He just took up and is holdin' on. The nesters have a legal right in here, an' Travers is square enough to admit it. He just don't like for 'em to be stealing him dry all the time. A steer now an' then for beef, sure. But not organized rustlin'."

They rode eastward along the bluff. A mile farther on the river made a sharp turn to the right and faded into the distance. Cic reined up and pointed that way.

"Our boundary line ends here, Jude. Over there is nester country. Them river lands and the prairies over there for miles is swarmin' with 'em. We've got line camps all along here—riders on the lookout fer stock that they keep pushin' back. But the cows slip through an' we never see 'em again. Then they make night raids while the line riders are asleep. By the way, Jude, you see thet shack about a mile down the turn of the river—down there among the mesquites an' the tall cottonwoods?"

Jude stood high in the stirrups of the new saddle, gun at his hip and the second one in the saddle sheath on the left fork. He nodded.

"That's Jim Harrison's place," Cic said. "Or rather it was," he finished awkwardly. "But come on; we've got work to do."

CHAPTER SEVENTEEN

THIS WAS the south boundary of Harry Travers' "holdings" and their job was to round up everything wearing his T4 brand and shove it back north, toward the grounds of the home ranch.

"We've got two line camps along here, spaced ten miles apart," Cic explained to Jude. "Two riders in each camp. They're supposed to patrol the line every day and push back everything they see wearing the boss's brand. One of the camps is about four miles west of here. But I never trusted Ernie Davis an' his pard Frank Jergens any too much. We shoulda run into 'em by now. You can see miles in this country when you get up on a rise, and we ain't seen 'em yet. Ten to one," he added sarcastically, "they're down at one of the stills some of these nesters run, guzzlin' raw corn whiskey an' making a deal to let the nesters slip by nights to run off T4 cattle."

"I thought a rider was supposed to be loyal to his outfit," Jude remarked.

That one brought a hard laugh from the scar-faced man riding beside him. "An honest puncher sticks by his outfit, Jude, come the devil and all his angels. He gets forty dollars a month and found, and for that he's supposed to stick by the boss. Most men do. But it's purty easy for a nester rustler to pay off a few dollars extra, or even split the profits, to have line riders workin' hand an' glove with them. There's some as'll even give the rustlers a hand. But I don't know fer sure; I'm only guessin'. I'm just telling you these things because you're out to make a puncher and you got to learn. But, hell—come on, look what I see down there."

What he saw was about thirty head of cattle grazing contentedly in a draw below them. They dropped down a sharp, winding cow trail and the wild cattle threw up their heads and began to trot off. The two riders followed them for a mile north and then wheeled back south again, toward the line. They worked on west, picking up scattered stuff here and there. By now they were a mile apart. About then Jude spotted an old bull with wide spreading horns, alone on a ridge among the mesquites. He was at least seven or eight years old and wore no brand.

One of the wary old brush boys that knew every foot of the country and had slipped through the roundups, Cic had told him about these. Down in south Texas, near the coast, they were known as mossy horns because they hid out in the timber and soon collected a growth of moss on their heads.

Jude spurred the blocky sorrel up over the ridge and the bull wheeled, disappearing into the mesquites. Jude went after him. He certainly had no intention of trying to rope and gotch *that* animal. He'd have tried to stop a locomotive first. But his orders had been to drive everything northward and Jude obeyed. The sorrel hunched into a run and they went smashing down through the mesquites, hard after the pumping haunches of the disappearing bull, its tail up over its back. Thorny limbs struck at his chaps and body and he threw up an arm now and then to protect his face. The bull was heading straight south, shooting for the bluffs and the underbrush of the river below. Jude worked dull rowels into the sorrel's pumping sides, and the animal that had thrown him twice proved its worth in a final burst of stamina that turned the fleeing longhorn and sent it crashing back to the north.

Jude kept after him hard, not giving him any chance to turn back. But he made the mistake of crowding the tiring animal too close. The next thing he knew two long horns were facing him at bay.

It was the sorrel that saved them both. It lunged to one side in time for one of the needle-tipped horns to miss its flanks by inches. Jude sat there in the saddle astride the heaving horse and watched the bull's lean rump disappear . . . south to its sanctuary along the river.

Lesson number one. Don't crowd a critter too close and put it on the prod.

He was learning fast.

He reined over and began jogging west again, wondering what had happened to Cic. Now and then he stopped to listen for the sounds of the other man working cattle out of the brush, but he heard nothing. Jude continued on along the line, dropping in and out of gullies that led toward the river. In one of these, choked with mesquites, he rode around a clump and saw Cic.

He saw the barrel of the rifle too. It was lined squarely at his chest from a distance of about fifteen feet.

Cic stood off to one side. His gunbelt was on the ground. There were two other men, including the man with the rifle. He was bearded, unwashed, and poorly dressed. He wore shoes instead of boots.

"All right, puncher," he snarled, baring yellow teeth. "Reach one han' down cautious like an' unbuckle that gunbelt an' let it drop to the ground. You make one other move an' I'll bore you with this Sharps."

Cic's voice cut in calmly, "You'd better do what he says, Jude. He was a good friend of Jim Harrison an' near as mean. This other coyote is Frank Jergens, who was supposed to be ridin' the line instead of helpin' slip them three cows an' calves across the river."

78

Jude looked at the renegade T4 puncher. He was ferret-toothed, shifty-eyed, a hard, grinning youth with a spine that curved into sloping shoulders. His gun was covering Cic.

"Move!" snarled the bearded nester with the Sharps.

Jude had come up with his left side to them. He reached with his right hand and unbuckled his gunbelt. It thudded to the ground.

"Now git down," ordered the man with the rifle. "So you're the smart younker who killed Jim Harrison, eh?" he sneered. "Well, you won't be killin' any more nesters. It's out fer you."

Jude leaned over and half lifted his leg as though to dismount, his hand unfastening the snap that held in place the sheath gun, his second gun, he had recently begun carrying in his saddle. Then he snatched it with a lightning move and shot across the neck of the sorrel. He killed the man with the Sharps, but the sorrel plunged and, with one leg out of the saddle, he hit the ground.

Jergens had spun, firing, his slow mentality making him panicky. Two shots struck the ground by Jude before he got lined. Then he shot Frank Jergens three times. The puncher went down in a crumpled heap. His legs began to thresh, the spur rowels making rattling sounds. Jude had snapped up, unaware that to Cic's amazed eyes he was a flaming-faced bundle of death, tawny as a puma and as chain-lightning fast; deadly as a striking rattlesnake.

Jergens was still threshing around on his back, leaving red smears on the ground. Blood was coming out of his mouth and he was making horrible choking sounds. Presently he shuddered and lay still while Jude stood like a stone statue, the long-barreled Smith and Wesson six-shooter still gripped in his hand. Then he lifted his face and spoke in a voice that Cic would never forget.

"I'm sorry I got separated from you, Cic. It was my fault, chasin' that mossy horn bull. You all right?"

Cic blew a great *whoosh* out of his lungs. "I'm all right. They got the drop on me. I was follerin' Tabor—thet's thet nester there—drivin' three cows an' calves toward the river, sneakin' up to ketch him red-handed. Then Frank slipped up on *me* and got the drop from behind. They were gettin' ready to make a cold-blooded job of it when we heard the sorrel."

He bent and picked up his gunbelt, strapping it on again. He rolled a cigarette and his fingers were trembling. Jude went to the sorrel some thirty yards away and led the sweat-covered animal back. It had been a hard run after that bull.

Cic said, to cover his shakiness, "You got to learn how to work a cow horse, Jude. He's like a man. He can sprint so far an' then he's got to be given a chance to blow an' get the trembles outa his legs."

Jude had shoved the death-dealing weapon back into the sheath and buckled the strap. He had shot with his left hand, thankful that he had done quite a lot of practising on the way down from Abilene. He might not have bothered had it not been for the fact that he remembered how Blackie had so dexterously handled a gun in his left hand. His and Blackie's trails had more or less parted, but Blackie was still his idol. So Jude had made excuses to go off into distant gullies, allowing the outfit to go on ahead; and when they were out of the sound of gunfire, the walls of a gully muffling the shots, he had pounded away first with one hand and then with the other.

But he knew that that first shot across the sorrel's neck, the shot that killed Tabor the nester rustler, was more luck than anything else.

"What do we do now?" he asked Cic.

"Leave 'em lay an' get back to the ranch. I've had enough work to last me fer today. Somebody'll have to go in town an' bring out the sheriff. But," he added, "you got nothin' to worry about. It was them or us."

"I could drift, I reckon. Plenty of room for a man over in Arizona Territory."

"You won't drift. There's no reason to. Jim don't like this rustlin' any more than we do. You've just saved him some extra work an' the T4 the Lord knows how many head."

CHAPTER EIGHTEEN

FOLLOWING Travers' orders that he fetch the sheriff, Slim Connors was burning the breeze across the flats. He disappeared into the mesquites beyond the gully, working his fresh mount with sure, skilled knowledge to get the utmost out of it on the fourteen-mile run to Alden. He was taking the short cut, not following the road.

He drove into town and, since he was a bronk stomper, his mount came first. He let it drink about half what it wanted at the town horse trough, took it over back of Sol's store, rubbed it down, and then walked it in a circle for fifteen minutes to let it cool off. He loosed the cinch, tied it at a corner of the wagon yard back of the store, and went in through the back. Sol was talking with a man when Slim came in—a nester.

Sol never took part in any discussions concerning the feeling between the rustling nesters and the cowmen.

The man was Red Tolliver.

"Hello, Slim," the merchant greeted him. "Never expected you to be in town at this time of day. Getting lazy?"

"Looking for the sheriff. Seen him around?"

"He went north this morning, up around Duck Creek. Somebody found a puncher of Henson's with a hole in his back. But Blackie's in the office. Anything up?"

"Plenty, Sol. That nester kid Jude an' Cic caught Tabor rustlin' three T4 cows this morning, with unbranded calves. Frank Jergens was with Tabor. They got the drop on Cic an' then on Jude. But that nester kid fooled 'em. He yanked a gun outa a sheath on his saddle an' started throwin' balls. He killed the both of 'em."

Slim enjoyed dispensing such important news.

"He killed who?" Sol demanded.

"Frank Jergens an' that nester Tabor. Tabor had the drop on him with a Sharps rifle, but Jude was too fast for him. He dropped him cold. Then he got Jergens."

Sol pursed his lips.

Red Tolliver said, through his lashless lids, "So Tabor's dead?"

Slim eyed him coolly. "Bored plumb center. Seems to me I recollect he was a good friend of yourn an' Harrison's."

His right hand lay close to his hip, fingers near the butt of his pistol. Tolliver had tensed. Sol saw it and pushed through between them.

"Cut it out!" he yelled. "This is a store, not a saloon. If you want gun fighting, go over to the saloons and do it."

Slim dropped his hand away from his belt. He turned his back on Tolliver and moved on toward the front door. Across the street the new red sandstone walls of the courthouse gleamed with color in the hot sun. Ahead of him was a sign that jutted out over the broadwalk. It said: *Sheriff's Office.*

Inside the office, Blackie sat back of the sheriff's desk, his booted and spurred feet up on the scarred top. He was leaning back in his chair, looking at Edwina. He was laughing softly, and the deputy sheriff's star on his breast gleamed brightly.

"All right," he was saying. "You're wonderful and I love you. But this is a big country and I've got plans. It's a new, fresh, raw country. It's growing. It's got room for men with vision and imagination . . . and I'm one of them."

She looked at him.

"No, Blackie," she said firmly, "you don't love me. You don't love anybody but yourself. There was a time when I would have given my life for you. I'd have lived with you in a brush and mud shack, had you said the word. But you didn't. All you wanted was for me to come with you to Alden. You made promises. I believed them. And now I know you for what you are. You're not fooling me, Blackie."

"You're talking in riddles," the deputy said sharply.

She shook her golden head. "Not riddles, Blackie. The truth. In a small town there are few secrets. I found out things I never realized were true."

"Yeah?" He was staring at her narrowly.

"You have more than four thousand dollars in the bank here in Alden," Edwina replied quietly. "I didn't love you for money. But when you came to Abilene, wrote me to meet you there, you didn't have money."

"I won at the wheel that night Jude and me shot it out with the dealer and he killed Harrison," he said in a hard voice.

"About eighteen hundred. You spent much of that despite the fact that you were gone from town for four days and I didn't know where you were."

He shifted his spurred boots to the floor. "What are you getting at?" he demanded harshly.

She smiled at him in a patient sort of way. "Just that this is the end for us, Blackie. I loved you enough to give up everything and follow you in the belief that you'd keep your promise of a marriage and a future out here. But not any more. I see you in your true light now. You never loved me. You never loved anybody but yourself. So it's all over. Where

82

you got that four thousand dollars you put in the bank I don't know nor will I ask. But this is the end for us."

She rose and he started to reply, but at that moment Slim Connors came in through the front door.

"Hello, Slim."

"Hello, Blackie. Howdy, miss," to Edwina. "Sol said Jim wasn't around."

"He's out of town, Slim," Blackie said. "What's on your mind?"

"Not much on mine, I reckon," he replied. "But plenty on the boss's an' Nute's. There was trouble on the south boundary this mornin'."

"Trouble?"

"Maybe it wouldn't exactly be called trouble," the bronk stomper replied. "From what I hear it happened too fast for that."

He explained about Tabor and Jergens, then added, "Their carcasses are down in a gulch ten miles south of the ranch. Travers wants the sheriff to burn the breeze out to the ranch. It's a twenty-four mile ride for you. But it looks like open war. Them nesters were out to git Jude an' for the second time he was a little too fast for 'em. I saw Red Tolliver in Sol's store just now. He seemed plumb upset when I told him about Tabor. Started to throw a gun on me."

Blackie had come up to his feet. Edwina looked at the bronk stomper. "Is Jude all right?" she asked.

Slim smiled at her patronizingly. "I reckon so. Nobody said anything when I left the ranch."

"I'll saddle a horse right away," Blackie said.

Slim pulled on the cigarette and let it drop between his fingers. "All right Blackie. That dun of mine is good for the return trip to the ranch. But I'm hongry. I'll eat an' meet you over back of Sol's store in about fifteen minutes."

He went out. Edwina looked at the deputy. "It's the end for us, Blackie."

He shrugged. "What are you going to do?"

"I have a little money and I know dresses and sewing. I'm going to open up a shop in town. I might be the town bad woman, but women can't resist dresses."

She went out and Blackie followed her. She turned toward Sol's store and he went along the north side of the square and into the livery barn and came out with his riding gear. Red

Tolliver swung down from his horse as the deputy was cinching up a long-legged claybank gelding.

"You hear the news?" Tolliver demanded sharply.

Blackie nodded, grunting as he notched the cinch and took the stirrup down off the horn. He turned to Red. "I'm riding out to make an investigation."

Tolliver's heavy, freckled face darkened. "I don't like it, Blackie. You said you'd swing that little sidewinder over on our side. I didn't mind him killin' Harrison. You were supposed to do that in Abilene to get him outa the way so's we could take over, but the kid beat you to it. That was all right, but this ain't. Tabor was the best man with a runnin' iron we got in the pool. You waited too long."

"I'm still running the show, Red," the deputy said coldly, "and don't you ever forget it. It's tough luck, all right, losing those two men. But Jude'll be worth any three Tabors if I can swing him."

"I'll tell the boys," Tolliver scowled. "They're whisperin' around themselves that this nester kid ain't a nester at all but a hired killer brought in by Travers."

Blackie swung up. He looked down at the big pot-bellied man with the two guns. "That's plain poppycock," he snapped. "I brought that kid into the outfit myself. Jude's all right. He'll do what I say. So pass the word along that he's in with us and to do no back shooting. I told you I was running this show. If we work it right the Nester Pool can put three thousand head up the trail next year. They got a Henson puncher over in the line camp on Duck Creek yesterday. It's a hint to Henson to sell out. I hear reports Travers is figuring on buying. When he does we'll have him spread out too thin. We can rustle him and the Circle C north of him dry. Savvy?"

Tolliver shrugged his bull shoulders. "All right, Blackie, just as you say."

"That's what I'm saying. And from now on don't ever be seen talking to me here in town unless we're quarreling and making threats."

He rode up back of the saloons, threaded his horse in between them, and presently Slim came out of the restaurant with a toothpick in his mouth. "I reckon we're ready to roll," he said, "soon's I git my hoss."

"No big hurry," Blackie said. "I can't get back to town tonight anyhow. I'll stay at the ranch."

CHAPTER NINETEEN

AFTER being interviewed by Blackie and exonerated of any wrongdoing, Jude wandered into the bunkhouse. Then Blackie's figure filled the open doorway. Greetings and exclamations rose. They bantered at him, gibed at him, jeered about the star on his shirt front.

"Take it easy, boys, I got somebody with me," Blackie smiled, and nodded toward the doorway. Nell had accompanied him down to the bunkhouse. An awkward silence fell.

Blackie said, "I just wanted to talk with Jude for a moment. Want to take a walk, Jude?"

"Sure," Jude replied, turning.

Mike and Cic and Slim Connors had risen simultaneously. Blackie caught the chill looks in their eyes and grinned.

"Jude's in the clear, boys. This is personal. Don't forget that he's my pardner."

Jude followed him out and the girl fell in beside them, Blackie gallantly taking her arm. They went over toward where the outlines of one of the huge freight wagons could be seen against the night sky.

They were at the wagon. Nell primly seated herself on the lowered wagon tongue where the doubletrees crossed its base and Blackie sat next to her. Jude took a seat and rolled a cigarette.

"What did you want to see me about?" he asked quietly.

"Not what you think. The Tabors and Jergens business is finished. You did what any good cowhand would have done. But the Nester Pool is out to get you, Jude. Every time you line a ridge you can expect a rifle shot. So I've got to protect you, Jude. I can do that in only one way."

"How?"

"By pinning a deputy sheriff's badge on you. You can work with me—Lord knows we need another man in the office. I can swing it with Jim. These nesters will give you a wide berth when you've a star on your shirt. They won't dare drop you

85

like they will now at the first opportunity. What do you say, pardner?"

Jude pulled on the half smoked length of the rolled cigarette. The red glow of the tip lit up his serious young face. He sent the butt sailing in a red arc into the darkness.

"Thanks for the offer, Blackie, but I want to learn the cow business. I can't do it, siding you with a reputation I don't deserve. I can't learn it hiding back of a lawman's badge. I'll stick here, I reckon, and take my chances."

"But you're refusing!" Nell Travers' indignant voice said in the darkness. "You can't do that!"

"Yes, I can," came the reply through the darkness. "I'm going to become a cowman, not an officer of the law. Thanks for the offer, Blackie. I appreciate it. I'll watch the ridges and if I have to high tail it, I'll do it."

He said good night and left them there on the wagon tongue, aware that Blackie's arm was around the girl and that he was making love to her.

Jude thought of Edwina in town and his jaw tensed.

It was the end of the T4 roundup.

They finished the branding and the beef cutout and moved northward, rounding up on the prairie within three miles of Alden. Shelby seemed to be everywhere at once, giving orders, directing operations, and seemingly always making marks in a tally book. Henson had ridden down with three of his men to drive back some thirty head of his stuff that had drifted south from Duck Creek. He was to begin his roundup in another week or ten days, and he and Travers and Shelby had been in serious huddles.

Right after the War Henson had established his iron and began putting it on all the unbranded stuff on the prairies, as other men all over Texas were doing.

Henson, an honest man himself, hadn't thought to devise an iron that would be tough on the brand blotters—and in that he differed very much from Travers. Travers' T4 was as hard to work over with a running iron as Henson's H Bar was easy.

And it had been the sharp-eyed Cic who had spotted the rebranded critter. Jude was with them when they roped and tied the animal. Shelby rolled it over on its other side, a husky two-year-old heifer.

He bent and parted the red hair, running his fingers over the freshly healed scab. The brand was an Eight Cross now.

"About two weeks ago, I'd say," he grunted to Henson. "A damned crude job, too. Any of them nesters up there running an Eight Cross iron?"

Henson shook his snow white head, a man of full seventy years old and still strong in the saddle. "Never heard of any, Nute. But then they come an' go an' sell out to each other all the time. Most of their brands ain't even registered."

"Probably not. Well, the man who did this job was either an amateur at the game or a puncher who was mighty careless. He probably drove the animal off the range an' then it got away from him an' drifted back. Looks to me like if you sell out to Harry we'll have our work cut out for us. Rustlers on the north and south boundaries with thirty miles of open range to draw from. What about your men?" he added sharply.

"All honest as far as I know, Nute. They don't go much for nesters."

Nute Shelby rose, freeing the animal's four tied feet. They all swung up.

"How's your tally showing up?" Henson inquired.

"Short," snapped the foreman. "A good three hundred head under what I estimated from the calf roundup last spring. And it's grown stuff. If Jim Underhill and Blackie don't put a stop to this rustling, I'm going to! I'll do it if I have to take a hundred men and burn every nester shack within fifty miles."

"That's one reason I'm selling out, Nute, I'm gettin' a mite old to be mixed up in a range war. The nesters are gettin' bigger all the time, even startin' a fair-sized outfit on what I allus figgered was my south range. But they've got as much legal right on that land as me an' the Missus have because it's free range."

"They haven't got any right on *mine!*" snapped out Travers. "I fought Indians in this country when there wasn't a town here. My mother is buried within four miles of here, her head split open with a Comanche tomahawk. I settled this range. I rode it as a kid, tending my father's ponies and keeping a sharp lookout for the red devils to top the ridges. Twice they chased me almost to the house at a run and then drove off the ponies. After the War I went south to where the cattle were thicker and fought tooth and nail to get my outfit going. I was so poor I couldn't even put a

87

herd up the trail until this year. This is my range and I'll fight to hold it."

"Come on, Nute. Let's go in town and have a talk with Jim Underhill and Blackie."

CHAPTER TWENTY

BOTH UNDERHILL and his deputy were in the office when the two men rode in.

"Hello, boys," the sheriff greeted them. "How's things going on the roundup? Looks like a lot of cows out there."

"A few," Nute said.

"Sit down, boys?" Blackie invited, nodding toward chairs. "How much longer will it take you to finish rounding up?"

Travers pushed back his hat as he sat down. "Not very long. And if those nesters keep rustling us at the rate they're doing we won't have enough left by next year."

"I know," Underhill put in. "I've got to play neutral and not take sides, but I'm personally for the cowmen. Yet you show me any proof that I can sink my teeth into and I'll go after any man, nester or puncher, who's rustling. I wish I had more help. One of us has to stay in the office most of the time and it's no easy job the way we're on the go. They haven't even got a town marshal here, so that means that after a man's rid a horse all day long he's got to spend a few hours makin' the rounds of the saloons to stop fights."

"Maybe we'd better talk to the commissioners and see about a couple of more deputies," Travers agreed. "Because if something ain't done about this rustling I'm going after them with guns. We're near three hundred head short on the tally so far since the calf roundup last spring. Prime stuff, most of it, with about sixty or seventy cows that should have big calves follerin' 'em being calfless. There's one roan cow in particular that I remember having a nice big bull calf with a white splotch on its shoulder. Her calf's gone. Three hundred head!"

Underhill whistled.

Shelby said in his curt voice. "But we've got to do something, Jim. We've got about seven thousand head of long horn cattle running on a range of about thirty miles. It's a big outfit and'll get bigger. I suppose you heard that Harry's taking over Henson's outfit on Duck Creek and adding it to the T4? Well, even an outfit that big can't stand being rustled at the rate we are. A few years of that, plus drouth or maybe a bad drop in prices, will put the T4 under as quick as though it was a small outfit. We'll buckle right in the middle."

Underhill sighed.

"You ever hear of an Eight Cross iron?" Travers demanded. Underhill shook his head. "New one on me."

He told about the job of brand blotting they had found on the Henson critter that day.

Blackie spoke up, reaching for cigarette papers and tobacco sack in the breast pocket of the red shirt.

"Eight Cross?"

"Yeah."

"I think that's an outfit just starting up about forty miles northwest of here, up in the Cap Rock country. Now that I'm packing this badge I can stop in at a nester's place for a drink of water without getting my head shot at."

"So you heard something?" grunted Shelby.

"Yes, I heard something, Nute," Blackie said slowly, looking at him steadily. "The nesters say that these big ranches the size of a Spanish land grant have to go—make room for smaller outfits. They say it's not right that a few big owners should have a two or three-hundred-mile stretch of open range, hogging up land they don't own and keeping the little fellows out. So the Eight Cross is being built. New bunkhouse and corrals. They got water up there and they're starting with about two hundred head, supposedly bought."

"Supposedly, hell!" exploded Travers, his face contorting with dark anger. "Half of those cows are either mine or Henson's! The others came from the big outfits far to the north. But it *is* a nester ranch, eh? You're sure?"

"Not only that," Blackie replied, licking the paper. "But down on your south boundary, Harry, Red Tolliver has pushed old man Dreddle back and just walked in and took over part of his grass. He bought out a couple of families that are going back to Missouri and moved the houses over to his own for bunkhouses. He's got five nesters riding for him as full time punchers, looking out after the pool stuff on that new range. You see what they're doing? First it was the Comanches on these prairies. They've been pretty well whipped out. Next you cowmen took over a range and held it. Now it's the nesters moving in—settlers, they call themselves—and shoving you out. It's not only happening here; it's happening all over the country. Nester kids are growing up who won't touch a plow. They ride horses. A new crop of punchers coming on, getting started like a lot of men got started—swinging a long loop on somebody else's stuff. And there's nothing on God's green earth you can do about it. You shoot one and another pops up like a steer outa the brush and takes his place. You've got about twenty-five men and they've got two hundred. If you make it open range war to see who survives, you'll go under."

The three had sat and listened to him, and it was pretty obvious from the thoughtful look on Travers' face that the shot had gone home.

"They'll never take my range. I'll hold it. I'll hold every foot of it if I have to hire a hundred punchers to ride it with rifles on the saddles."

"Well," shrugged Blackie, "it's your ruckus, Harry. We'll back you as far as the law and our limited means will go. But you're fighting men who were at Bull Run and Gettysburg and Atlanta with rifles in their hands. Men from both sides who can, and will, kill. You've bucked a stacked deck, Harry."

Travers got up and paced the room worriedly.

"I could make a suggestion," Blackie smiled up at him. "It might be a way out. I don't want to make it on account of knowing how touchy you are about the range."

"What is it?"

"It's better to play safe and lose some than to buck a deck and lose more. I'd suggest that you let me arrange to meet with a committee of nesters from the south and a committee over on your north and west boundaries. Pull back a few miles and cut a boundary and agree to let them get started. They—"

"Hell no!" exploded Travers angrily. "Give 'em an inch and they'd crowd a foot."

"Then buy your land and establish definite ownership."

Travers stared at him aghast. "Buy it?" he roared. *"Buy it?* Did the Comanches pay anything for it? Are the nesters payin' anything for it? Hundreds and hundreds of miles of open range all over Texas, free for the taking, and I'm supposed to *pay* for it! Gawdlemighty, I never heard of anything so dam' silly in all my life, spending money for *land!*"

Blackie's wiry shoulders shrugged. "All right, Harry, I won't say any more. But that's what the new Eight Cross outfit is doing, getting title to land for a few pennies an acre. They've had surveyors on your northwest range and the line will run about three miles inside what you figure is your boundary. They're buying *your* range with the money they got from that rustled NP herd they took to Abilene. They bought a hundred and sixty acres on the place where they're putting up the ranchhouse. They're spreading their money thin, leaving all the land in between. I know all this for a fact because since I've been packing this badge I've got around quite a bit. I've learned things. When the deeds come through from the State Land Office they'll own part of your range."

"The devil they will! The first nester who crosses that boundary will get his head shot off. I'll go up there with a dozen men and burn that place down."

Blackie got up, his eyes cold. Travers didn't know it, of course, but it was Blackie himself who was the Eight Cross.

"When you do, Harry, the State of Texas'll say that Jim and myself will have to come after you with a warrant for your arrest."

He got up and went out, strolling up the street. Red Tolliver stood leaning against a doorjamb with his big belly protruding past the wall. There was nobody around and Blackie paused briefly.

"I just saw Travers an' Nute Shelby in town a little while ago," Red said, his lashless lids opaque.

"They're in the office, considerably upset over a three-hundred-steer and calf shortage. And one of Henson's drifters showed up in the T4 roundup with a brand made over into an Eight Cross so crudely, it looked like even the kids are trying their hand at rustling. Tell those fools to be careful!"

Tolliver grinned. "Sorta upset, hey?"

"Travers? Plenty. But we've got him worried and just about where we can start to work."

The rustler grinned. "Yo're near as much of a plain blackguard as I am, Blackie."

Blackie smiled at that one. "More so, Red. *You're* an honest one!"

91

CHAPTER TWENTY-ONE

JUDE AND CIC joggled into town around three o'clock in the afternoon the day after Travers bought the H Bar holdings. They would stop in the store and buy heavy coats and winter underwear and other necessities for a winter alone in a line camp. Shelby had chosen wisely in having the older man accompany Jude. Putting two men of the same age and temperament in a cabin for an entire winter was often tantamount to inviting death for one of them. "Cabin fever" was a tough problem for any foreman. Two men cooped up together night after night got tired of one another's tall tales, repeated over and over again, the drone of the same voice, the shape of the same head. Many a pair had come out in the spring, once former close friends, and now bitter enemies. The two punchers went in through the back of Sol's store to start buying. Cic and Jude made their purchases—on credit until spring—bought two quarts of whiskey at the saloon next door, and rode out of town.

They wintered on the far tip of the former Henson range, in a shack that was divided into two rooms, one for bunking and one for cooking. The shack was on a bare knoll, with the sheds for the horses down below in the lee of the crest. The horses would need all the protection they could get when the wind howled and the sleet came driving down slantingly.

In a matter of days they settled into line camp life. It was a matter of getting up about daylight, feeding the horses and cooking breakfast, and then bundling up for the long cold ride to push all the Henson stuff south and to prevent nester stuff, driven by the cold, from drifting over onto the new T4 range. Now and then Jude met hard-eyed men on the same job, their small holdings visible far to the north; men who rode by cautiously, at a distance of a hundred yards, eying the T4 man warily, and sometimes lifting a gloved hand in a curt greeting. Once a month Joe, bundled up against the bitter cold, drove by in the bedroll wagon, loaded down with supplies for the camps. He usually stayed overnight, exchanged and passed along the latest gossip.

Things were going pretty well at the home ranch and in town. The winter range was in pretty good shape so far, the cattle holding up well. Travers figured that, with the addition of Henson's spread to his holdings, he could put four thousand head up the trail next summer. The furniture for the new house was being freighted in by the two big wagons and everybody was looking forward to the barbecue and general celebration when the weather warmed up a bit.

It was a good winter, Jude thought. He lay in his bunk nights and listened to the wind and thought about Edwina. He began to get ideas that perhaps he might drift. This was in mid-January.

Then things changed. Joe started it when he broke the news on one of his monthly trips: Jim Underhill, the sheriff, had been found two weeks before up on the edge of the nester country fifteen miles west of Jude's section of the line. He had been dead about a week. A nester had found his horse wandering half-starved and frozen, and had back tracked.

The sheriff had been shot through the back with a rifle. Blackie was now acting sheriff and had hired two new deputies. What made it worse, Joe swore profanely, was that they were both nesters.

Jude was genuinely sorry about the death of the sheriff. Underhill had been a good man.

"So Blackie's gone over to the nesters, eh?" Cic grunted. He reached over and lit a cigarette from the top of the lamp glove on the table. The three of them had just eaten supper and were in the kitchen of the cabin.

"I wouldn't say that," Joe replied. "He said as how he didn't much want the job. But there wasn't anybody else."

"He coulda hired a couple of good gun-packin' punchers!" snapped Cic.

"I reckon he could," the limping man agreed. "But what you boys don't realize is that Alden is becoming a nester town. Travers is the only big ranchman there, most of the others freightin' from further north an' west. An' these nesters have all got cows now, too. I hear that new Eight Cross outfit added four hundred more head."

"Yeah?" grunted Cic narrowly.

"Yep. An' that ain't the worst part. Their surveyors drawed up a line several miles inside what was part of Travers' range juttin' on to Henson's. An' they bought all thet land legal-like. Owsley—he's the new foreman an' he ain't no nester, though he's got nester punchers—says as how come spring an' his Eight Cross stuff will be headin' right over onto thet new grass. He told Travers plain in Sol's store one day thet he didn't want to see any T4 or H Bar irons on thet grass when they come over with their own stuff."

"What did the boss say?" Jude asked. That disputed land was a part of his assigned line.

The crippled little ex-rider grinned at that one. "Whut would you expect him to say, Jude? He told Owsley an' them four hard nester punchers with him thet his men would shoot the first cow an' the first rider thet crossed the old boundary."

"Them's our orders?" Cic cut in.

Joe nodded. "I got word fer you two to sorta follow 'em accordin' to how you feel."

"Well, I reckon thet makes it plain enough," the older puncher grunted.

That was the first ominous portent of trouble coming on the range. Joe had said that Texas Rangers were drifting in. They had investigated the death of the sheriff, but by the time they arrived at the spot where the body had been found an overnight rain had obliterated all tracks of the man who had drygulched the officer.

Jude went back to his riding, and the worst part of a bad Texas winter closed down in February. They fought it out, he and Cic, riding when they could and pushing the humped up cattle into draws, trying to hold them against the storm until it abated and then drive them back over onto the nesters' holdings. It snowed four inches in late February, followed by another of those miserable driving northers that froze the snow to hard crusted ice, and the effects of it showed on the cattle. Quite a large number of the older, poorer cows froze to death in the draws during those final two nights when Jude and Cic sat humped over the smoking stove in the kitchen and tried to keep warm. They had to use saddle blankets over their tarps, and they slept in their clothes.

When the wind died down the following morning and the sun came out warm, Jude rode across the white-covered land and was appalled by what he saw in the choked draws. If it had been like that on the south range, down below the home ranch, then Harry Travers certainly wouldn't be putting any four thousand head up the trail next year—or the following. It turned Jude sick to see the dead young calves.

But the weather had given all in that final storm and it began to turn warm. The grass began greening overnight and it became muddy. Jude rode with jerky beef and cold biscuits in his saddlebag and was out all day. He was still leaner than before and his hair was down over his ears in shaggy locks. He and Cic had gotten along fine during the lonely, hard months.

They laughed and joked and played crude tricks on each other and then went out to work the day through, sometimes not getting back until dark. But the nester country to the north of them wasn't such good range and their cattle always appeared to have a penchant for the grass farther south. Then it finally dawned on Jude that they were not drifting; they were being driven! The nesters were encroaching. It was deliberate.

Thus it came about that one morning Jude rose two hours earlier than usual. He left Cic sound asleep in his bunk, drank a cup of coffee, and picked up the food he had prepared the night before. He hadn't told Cic what he was going to do. The older man would have insisted on changing places with him. Jude closed the door softly behind him and went down to saddle up. Daylight found him eight miles west of the line cabin. He rode on, topped a ridge, and then he saw them: three nesters working forty or fifty head of their stuff over onto what had been the old Henson range. Jude put spurs to his mount and loped forward to the west.

The three had seen him and then pulled up, as though uncertain. Jude pulled up too, three hundred yards away.

"Put 'em back!" he yelled. "Don't let 'em cross."

"This is nester land now, cowpunch. They'll cross," came back an answering call.

Jude bent in the saddle and brought up his rifle. It was a .44-40 repeater, model of 1866. He swung his horse around so that its left side faced the oncoming cows. Coolly he fired. A cow dropped. He dropped two more. A yell went up and a shot banged over his head. He slapped steel to the horse and buck-jumped it into an arroyo and then swung down, crawling back to the top of the ridge while he thumbed shells from his belt into the magazine. But the three riders had disappeared.

Jude shoved the gun back into its sheath and remounted.

He drove the cows back, watched them amble into the brush, and rode on along the line. When he got back that afternoon and told Cic what had occurred the older man was furious.

"Why didn't you tell me?" he demanded harshly. "You mighta got yourself killed! I'd have gone with you."

"You've got your end of the line to ride, in the other direction, Cic," Jude said quietly.

A shadow had darkened the doorway. The man who stood there was about thirty-five years of age. He wore a brown hat, checkered shirt, dark wool pants, and boots that came to the knee, big "ears" flopping at the tops. Jude gave these a cursory glance. He wasn't interested in either the clothes or the guns the man wore, but in the keen face and his badge. The badge had the words *Texas Ranger* stamped into it.

"Come in," he invited.

The man came in. He took off his hat, glancing around the kitchen. "Howdy, boys," he greeted them in a soft voice not in keeping with his appearance. "I'm Durton. Texas Rangers. Which one of you men was riding east end of the line from the camp this morning?"

"Him," Cic said belligerently. "Why?"

The Ranger looked at Jude. "You shot some Lazy S cows."

Jude nodded. "Three men driving them across over onto our range. I warned them not to. They said it was nester range now. I dropped three head and then ducked when one of them let drive at me with a rifle."

"Hmm. They didn't say anything about *thet* part of it. But they claim they've bought this range an' are entitled to graze it."

"I've been riding that line every day since last fall," Jude told him quietly. "There were no surveyors on it before I came and there weren't any during the winter. They've supposedly surveyed and bought further west and south, toward Cap Rock, where the Cross Eight has set in, but not down here."

"I saw your trail cut out of the grass during the winter," the Ranger admitted. "And I talked to Henson before I came up. No surveyors, eh?"

"None," snapped Cic, still belligerent. "Seems to me you put in a purty quick appearance here, mister, after Jude drove them cows off. You in with these damned nesters?"

"The Rangers," came the quiet, hard reply, "ain't in with anybody. But there's rumors you've got a range war brewing between Travers an' the small cowmen and, mister, that range war just ain't going to take place."

"And just how did you git holt of all these 'rumors' you're talkin' about?"

"We had word from the acting sheriff here," the other explained patiently. "Blackie Hepburn. He sent in word to headquarters there was trouble brewing and some of us were sent down." He looked at Jude. "All right, son, there'll be no action taken because of this ruckus this mornin' seein' the legality of these small cowmen's claims are in doubt. I reckon I'd have done the same thing in your boots if I was back punchin', like I used to do. But just be a little more careful."

Cic thawed a little and invited him to stay for supper. They had beans with big chunks of fat pork cooked in them, boiled potatoes, canned corn, and some cooked dried fruit, topped off by the inevitable cups of black coffee.

The Ranger rose with a sigh of contentment.

"That was a good meal, boys. Travers seems to feed his hands well." He struck a match on the still warm stove, lit the rolled cigarette, and reached for his hat. "Well, I'll be going. Thanks for the supper."

He rode out, swung aboard his horse, and disappeared into the night along the trail Jude had ridden westward almost every day for months.

Two days later Jude found his body.

CHAPTER TWENTY-TWO

HE SAW the saddled horse first, about nine o'clock that sunny morning. It was wandering with reins dragging. He rode over and grabbed up the dangling reins, noting the bloodstains on the saddle. They were fresh and so were the tracks of the animal. Durton lay less than three hundred yards away.

Jude swung down and looked at the dead man. The Ranger had half rolled over on his side. He hadn't been killed quite instantly. Smoke rose from a fire down below, and Jude went down the slippery bank.

It was a branding fire. Of that there could be no doubt. Cow and calf tracks led up over the bank, and Jude went for his horse. He mounted and began following them. They led north, straight across the boundary into nester country, as he had known they would. Jude looked back at the spot where the horse now stood. He followed the tracks.

He crossed over and spurred along the trail, for Durton hadn't been dead more than an hour. Jude kept a sharp lookout for signs of movements. He was in the enemy's domain now.

Presently he pulled up, lipped a ridge cautiously, and saw his quarry. The rustler was a quarter of a mile ahead, driving a cow and calf ahead of him and urging them to greater speed.

Jude swung to the east, ducked back of a ridge that ran down close to Duck Creek's westward curve, and spurred hard. The soft sand took up the muffled beat of his horse's hoofs. He circled, cut in back of another promontory and swung down with his .44-40 in hand. The rustler rounded the promontory, throwing uneasy glances back of him.

It was Grady.

"Get 'em up!" snapped Jude. "Up, Grady, or I'll blow you apart. I mean it!"

Grady saw the levelled barrel of the repeater and slowly obeyed, panic in his face.

"Howdy, Jude," he said in a whining voice. "What you doin' over here in nester country?"

"You know damn well what I'm doing. Drop that gunbelt with your right hand, Grady, and don't make any false moves."

Grady obeyed. Jude's eyes had gone to the cow and calf. It was one of Henson's H Bar cows, but the calf bore a newly burned Eight Cross on its hip. The Ranger had surprised him. The cow would either have been shot or driven further north to have her brand blotted. Jude rode closer.

"Aw, hell, Jude, Travers has got plenty of cows; he won't miss a calf now an' then," Grady protested.

"He's missing plenty of them, but that's not what counts. I found the Ranger you shot, Grady. Now round up that cow and calf and get 'em started south. You're not packing a saddle gun, and if you try to make a break for it I'll drop you."

They got going, driving the rustled cow and calf before them, with Jude looking back over his shoulder. He had the evidence that would help to strengthen Travers' case against the nesters, and he didn't want a fight on his hands. They crossed back over the boundary and came to where the dead man lay. And about that time Cic came loping up.

"Just a hunch I had," he said quietly. "Just a hunch, Jude. Figgered you might get a shot in the back. Hello, Grady. So you're in with the nester pool now, eh?"

Grady maintained a sullen silence while Jude explained what had happened.

"Now," Cic grunted angrily, "I know who rattled thet slicker thet night up on Gramma Crick in Kansas an' shot Tolson in the dark. The pool had some of their men waiting for whatever we lost in the stampede."

Grady said hoarsely, "Cic, I swear I didn't stampede that herd that night. I swear it! I was clean over on the other side of the herd an' I think I kin prove it. I was tryin' to turn 'em. One of the other boys was with me close by, an' if he ain't drifted he'll tell you the same. I didn't rattle that slicker. It was somebody else. I was doin' my best to help out, like as how any good puncher should. I was all for the T4 until Nute fired me in Abilene. Then I come back here all mad at Nute an' threw in with the nesters."

Something in his frantic words held the ring of truth. Jude didn't think that Grady was lying this time. He said, "That'll all come out later. Right now we got a dead man on our hands, plus a rustled cow and calf. What do we do now, Cic?"

Cic's eyes glinted as he rubbed his scarred jaw. "Go in with 'em," he said. "We can make Alden by dark if we push hard enough. I want Blackie an' every dam' Texas Ranger in these parts to see this. Maybe it'll show 'em who's doin' the rustlin'. Let's get Durton's body lashed on his hoss."

They lashed the dead man face down across his saddle and started driving the cow and calf ahead of them. But progress was slow and presently Jude said to Cic, "One of us oughta ride ahead and get Blackie. What do you think?"

"Good idea. You're lighter'n me, not to speak of bein' a hell of a lot younger. My bones don't take the jolts so good any more. I'll keep pushin' this cow an' calf directly across country, an' takin' care of Grady, the dam' brand-burnin' nester! You burn the breeze on in an' come back with some help. They'll hang Grady for killin' thet Ranger."

"I still didn't stampede that herd," Grady protested.

Jude gave Cic a wave of the hand and turned in the saddle,

99

heading southward. His weight was slightly less than one hundred and fifty pounds and the cow pony beneath him had been loafing for two days. He sent it forward at a long lope.

It was drenched with sweat when he finally swung down before Bronson's stable.

He walked southward toward the line of saloons, came in between two of them, and turned west toward where the sheriff's office had been. The sign above the clapboard building was gone. A man came along the street; recognized him; one of the original Henson punchers, now on the T4 payroll.

"You're thet line rider from over on Duck Creek, ain't you?"

Jude nodded. The newly finished courthouse gleamed red in the sun and so did the new stone jail.

"Seen the sheriff around?" Jude asked.

"Blackie? Sure. Just come from the courthouse. Thet's his office on this corner. Things kinda changed around here since you left, boy. We're growin' up."

"Thanks," Jude said brusquely, and left him. He went across into a big hallway running north and south through the building, with doors leading off on either side. One said *County Treasurer* in bold letters. Others said *County Attorney, County Clerk, County Judge.*

One Jude hadn't noticed said *County Sheriff.*

No doubt about it. Alden was coming up.

He saw three men. One of them was Blackie. The two others were Texas Rangers. Blackie dropped his feet from his desk, a look of pleasant surprise coming over his face. "Well, look who's here," he greeted Jude, getting up and extending a hand. "Hello, Jude, boy, I'm glad to see you. Thought it would be another couple of weeks before Harry relieved his winter line riders. You're early."

Jude shook hands with him, and Blackie introduced him to the Rangers, Renner and Hardin.

"Travers didn't relieve Cic and me," Jude said.

"Trouble?" asked one of the Rangers; the younger one.

"Trouble," Jude said.

"We got a man up that way, Durton. You seen him?"

"Cic's bringing him in," Jude answered. "Seems as though he caught one of the nesters branding a calf and got shot." He looked at Blackie. "It's Grady. I caught him red-handed. Cic's bringing *him* in too. I came on ahead to get you."

100

Blackie was eyeing him. "Grady? What's he doing back in this country after Nute fired him in Abilene?"

"It kind of looks like he's rustling cattle."

"A branded calf, you say? What brand?"

"Eight Cross on the calf. H Bar on the cow. I got the drop on him and back traced to where he had killed Durton. Cic came up and started to bring them in—Durton's body, the two critters, and Grady. Grady swears it wasn't him that stampeded the herd that night up on Gramma Creek, in Kansas. I believe what he said."

The two Texas Rangers looked at each other. "I reckon we better get rolling," the hard-faced one said.

Then Travers came in the doorway and stopped to look at Jude. More crisp explanations were necessary. Blackie was buckling on his guns and picking up a pair of handcuffs.

"I reckon I'll go with you, boys," Travers said. "What do you Rangers think now?" the cattleman asked brusquely.

"We don't think," came the reply from the hard-faced man. "We just act."

Jude said, "My horse is tired and I'm hungry. You should meet Cic not more than seven or eight miles out. You need me to go with you?"

"No," Blackie replied. "We'll find them. You wait in town and get some rest and we'll be in before sundown."

Jude watched them go, the two Rangers to mount their horses, Travers to get his from in back of Sol's store, Blackie to pick up one from Bronson's livery. Jude went across the square to a restaurant. He ate and then got a haircut and lounged around town. He was waiting for the reappearance of the four men and what Cic was bringing.

He wanted to go to see Edwina, but some instinct kept him from doing so. He carefully avoided that section of the street where her shop was located.

Five men came in at about an hour before sundown. The two lawmen, the sheriff, Travers, and Grady. Grady wore a pair of handcuffs now, and was a badly frightened puncher. Jude was at the Bronson livery corral when they drove in the cow and calf, each wearing different brands. The cow was angry and the calf was hungry. It went for its mother and began sucking, the newly burned brand on its hip showing up plainly. Jude saw the grim look on Blackie's face as he and the two Rangers took the frightened Grady over to the new jail. They came out again, swinging shut the iron door.

101

Travers hadn't accompanied them. He had put away his horse, exchanging it for a borrowed fresh one to make the return ride to the ranch, and now he rode over to where Jude and Cic stood.

"Here comes the boss," the older man said.

"How'd he take it?" Jude asked.

"He made the most of it. He lit into them Rangers like you never saw before. Told 'em off plenty about nester rustlin'. They didn't say much."

Little knots of men were clustered on corners. Nester women came out of the store and stood looking. A man wearing a bartender's apron stood on the boardwalk on the north side of the square, staring, watching the dead Ranger.

Travers reined up. He looked down at the two T4 men. "I'll send a couple more of the boys up to the camp to take over," he said. "You two can come on back to the ranch. Want to stay in town tonight?"

"Sounds good," Jude replied.

"This is a big town for a pilgrim from a winter line camp but I'll try to make out," Cic answered.

"All right. Stay in and kick up your heels. But we've got work to do and visitors coming to the ranch. Somebody'll have to meet 'em. See you boys at the ranch."

CHAPTER TWENTY-THREE

THEY WENT over to the hotel and got rooms. Joe was due at the line camp in a day or so with his wagon and would bring their tarps and other stuff back to the ranch. Cic and Jude went out for a couple of drinks. The bar next to Sol's big store was pretty well filled with men.

"Nesters," grunted Cic in an aside, and spat.

Men looked at them and either stared or silently turned away. Others looked coldly and then resumed conversation, ignoring them. Not much doubt about it: Alden was becoming a nester town. They were the only two regular punchers in the place.

One of them Jude recognized. He was a man with a short-cut yellow beard, the hair trimmed spade-like across the bottom of his chin. The man was big, hard-eyed, belligerent-looking.

"What'll it be, boys?" the bartender asked.

"Rye," Cic said. "I got to cut the taste outa my mouth."

"It looks," a voice said distinctly and sneeringly, "like a small cowman cain't come in an' have a drink any more without the place bein' smelled up with mesquite an' horse sweat an' horse dung. Somebody orta open the window."

Cic turned slowly, eyeing the speaker. It was the man with the yellow spade-shaped beard. Jude was pretty sure he and his two friends made up the trio who had driven the cows across the old Henson north boundary that other morning.

It became dead quiet in the room. The bar was bare except for a line of glasses containing unfinished drinks, and five men. Jude and Cic were at one end and the three nesters at the other. The bartender brought the drinks. His hands were trembling as he placed bottles and glasses.

Jude reached into a shirt pocket, where he happened to have some change. He used his left hand. The right lay close to the butt of his six-shooter. Cic picked up the bottle.

"It's plumb awful what a winter in a line camp will do for a feller," he said. "He gits outa touch with civilization. He fergits things. Now you take me: I ain't heard hooman voices in so long I've sorta fergot what they sound like. I thought fer a minute I heard somebody speak, but I recognize it now. It was one of the town jackasses out in the alley, a-brayin' an' a-hee-hawin'. It wasn't a hooman at all." He drank with a backward flick of his head pouring another after he wiped his lips. "Sure cuts the bad taste an' sound outa a man," he remarked.

"Was you the fellers found thet Ranger this mawnin'?" Yellow Beard asked sarcastically.

Cic looked at the bartender. "It's that jackass again," he complained. "A-brayin' an' a-hee-hawin'. Cain't you go out in the alley an' chase him away, Johnny? I been up in a line camp so long my hearin' is plumb sensitive. Tell you what, Johnny," to the rigid, frozen-faced barkeep. "I'll loan you my rope. You double it an' go out an' bust him on the rump an' chase him up back of Sol's store. Sol's a purty kind-hearted feller. He's even kind to nesters. You tell him I said give this burro a bale of hay an' I'll pay fer it. I'll bet he's been so hongry fer a real good meal of hay that he's been forced to eat T4 *beef* to keep alive."

There could have been no more direct insult and every man in the room knew it. A man cleared his throat uneasily and Jude's cold eyes flicked to him, flicked back to Yellow Beard's sneering face.

He switched his attention to Jude.

"How's the cow-shootin' business these days?" Yellow Beard inquired blandly.

"Not very good," Jude answered quietly. "I had plenty of chances but I hate to shoot our own stuff."

"Was yuh very upset over them three pore critters yuh downed?"

"I was more upset over that try you made at me with a rifle. You ought to spend some of that beef money buying some cartridges and practicing."

"I got plenty of cartridges."

"Then," jeered Cic, "why don't you use 'em an'—"

It happened then. Jude had caught the downward jerk of the yellow-bearded man's shoulder. Two six-shooters came up over the bar almost simultaneously. The nester's gun roared and Cic grabbed frantically at the bar as Jude's own gun smashed back in recoil against his palm. He drove a .44 slug straight into the beard, shot the second man, and killed the third as the nester fired wildly. Three bodies thudded to the floor and Jude grabbed out with his left arm, Cic's weight sinking into it.

"Don't move!" Jude snarled, his gun covering the others. "I'll kill the first man who makes a move."

He stood, flaming-faced, the smoking six-shooter in his right hand. He pushed Cic over to rest his weight against the bar and Cic fumbled for the bottle. Red was beginning to stain the left shoulder of his shirt.

"What I need is a drink," he mumbled. "Johnny, ain't you got no manners?" His gun was still in its sheath; the nester with the beard had shot without warning.

The heavy sounds of the six-shooters had blasted out through the open doors and into the town. Jude heard yells and running feet. Men began to pour in. The first three in were Blackie and the two Texas Rangers.

Jude was still supporting Cic's sagging figure, while Cic was still mumbling and trying to hold onto the bar.

Three dead men lay on the floor, one of them still twitching. Red smeared into the sawdust.

"Put that gun down!" Blackie roared at Jude.

"I'll put it down when those nesters get their hands in sight."

"I said put it down!"

"Keep out of line of fire, Blackie," Jude said tonelessly. "They got Cic without warning. His gun is still in the sheath. Theirs are on the floor."

"'Here, son," the older Ranger with the hard face interrupted.

He hauled Cic over to a table and sat him down in a chair. Cic fell forward across the green top, face resting on his elbows.

Slowly Jude sheathed the six-shooter. Blackie was staring at him. He asked, "What happened?"

Jude jerked his head toward the barkeep. His flaming young eyes were still on the frozen men at the tables.

"Ask him. Tell him, Johnny. Tell him exactly what happened."

The barkeep told them. "Porter," he finished, nodding toward the yellow-bearded man on the floor, "jerked his gun first and shot Cic an' was linin' at Jude when Jude got 'im. The other two drawed—their guns are clear of the sheaths an' on the floor—but Jude killed the three of 'em with three shots. He had that gun out so fast I hardly seen it."

Blackie looked at Jude, who still stood by the bar. He saw a young face that was pale but containing no fear. Six men now. Six men gone out of the nester pool. And those three guns on the floor, Cic's gun still in its sheath—

Blackie looked at the Rangers and Jude saw uncertainty in his eyes. Blackie was thinking in that moment that Jude had to go. Give this quiet-eyed young ex-farmer time and he'd wipe out the pool.

The younger of the Rangers had stepped forward, looking down at the three dead men. He bent and picked up Porter's gun, examining it.

"One shot fired," he said. "Thet was the one thet got that other puncher whose gun is still in the sheath. The others didn't shoot?" he asked the barkeep.

"They didn't have time," Johnny answered. "Cornell was drawing when Jude got him. Broden's gun was up over the bar when he got it square in the face."

"Well, Blackie?" queried the hard-faced Ranger.

"What do you think?" Blackie returned. "Looks like I'll have to arrest Jude."

"Arrest, hell! It was self-defesne—and ain't you kind of forgettin' that this young puncher got the rustler who shot Durton when he surprised him rustlin' a cow and calf?"

"All right," Blackie looked at Jude. "You're in the clear, Jude. But you're doing all right for yourself. You've got six notches on your gun. That's a hell of a lot of men for a puncher not turned twenty yet. But as acting sheriff I warn you, Jude: if this keeps up, I'll have to bring you in one of these days."

"We better get a doctor for Cic," was the quiet reply.

"I'll get one," one of the Rangers said. And to Jude: "Son, we can use a man like you before you throw a gun at the wrong time an' end up as a desperado. It'll happen sooner or later if you keep this up. No wild shooting cowpuncher can last. He either goes to boothill or he hangs. It's better to be on the side of the law than on the other side. I'll talk to you again soon."

"Thanks," Jude said, and went to Cic.

Two women pushed through the crowd jammed at the front door. They were Edwina and Nell Travers.

"Oh, Jude, I'm sorry," Edwina cried out.

"It's all right," he answered.

Nell had gone to Cic, still down over the table, his face buried in his arms. He was unconscious from the shock of the big bullet. She got him in her arms, pulled him from the chair, and stretched him out on the floor, unbuttoning his blood-soaked shirt. "Get me some clean bar towels," she called out.

She was still working over him when the doctor arrived. A borrowed knife had cut away the shirt. Cic lay with his chest bared, red trying to ooze through the pads she had put on.

The doctor—his name was Vogel—got busy. He strapped Cic's chest tightly to stop the flow of blood and rose.

"One of you men go get a light wagon and we'll take him down to my house," he commanded. "I'll have to probe for the bullet and remove it. It missed the lung. Lodged above it."

He went over to the bar and poured himself a drink into one of the glasses. He turned and surveyed the crowd, a disillusioned-looking man of about forty-five. "Gun fighters," he said. "Wild, gun-throwing cow-punchers who pack six-shooters and kill at the slightest provocation. I served four years as a surgeon in the Confederate Armies. I patched them up, I amputated, I stood over them and watched them die, some of them boys not more than fifteen, their guts blown out by rifle and pistol balls. Three hundred and fifty thousand of them from the South. Two hundred and fifty thousand more from the North. And for what? For the survivors to come out here, guns still on their hips, rifles in their hands, and continue the slaughter. I wish to God I had become either an atheist or a minister—anything but a doctor. Man's inhumanity to man!" He poured himself another drink. On the floor Cic lay still, faint groans coming from deep within his tortured chest.

Jude found himself out into the clean air of the street. He found the two women walking alongside him. Nell broke the silence.

"I came in to get fitted for some new dresses for the house-warming," she said to Jude. "We're making the final ones to-night. Edwina and I have become good friends since you left."

"I'm glad," Jude said. And to Edwina: "Are you coming out for the celebration?"

Nell laughed. "Of course she is, silly! So is Sol and everybody else in town. Well, a lot of them."

"When is it to be?"

"Saturday night—two days from now. My guests from the East will be in on the stage Saturday morning. Pa's already had the barbecue pits dug and is going to butcher a steer. The house is all finished."

They stopped in front of Edwina's place and the two women went in. Jude walked on toward the hotel. He wasn't hungry any more. All he wanted to do was to go up to his room and lie down. He saw a man across the street, at the hitch rack in front of the dance hall; a potbellied man who wore two guns.

Red Tolliver.

CHAPTER TWENTY-FOUR

JUDE WAS DRESSED and washing his face in a big white bowl on the bureau the next morning when Blackie came in.

"Morning, Jude," the deputy greeted him.

"Morning."

"How do you feel?"

Jude reached for the towel, drying his face and damp hair.

"I didn't sleep very well, Blackie. Kind of tossed around."

Blackie smiled and seated himself on the edge of the rumpled bed. The covers were twisted and slantwise with a corner of a quilt down on the floor. He rolled a morning smoke. Jude bent to the mirror, parting his fine hair.

"I don't blame you. That was some fracas. But I felt the same way first time I ever shot it out with a man. You come on down and have breakfast with me."

"All right. I've got to get back to the ranch this morning. But you never have said just how many men you have downed, Blackie, and I never asked, though I was always a bit curious." He picked up his hat and then swung the heavy cartridge belt around his slim waist. It slid into place.

They went out.

"Four, Jude," the sheriff replied as they went down the hallway to the steps. "That is, not counting the war."

"I never heard you say anything about the war."

Blackie grinned. "You won't either. It's only been over four years and Texas was on the losing side. You see, Jude, I was a Union spy, working back of the Confederate lines. Spying is not the most honored profession among the men who fought on both sides. But somebody had to do it, and I did; and a few times when I was found out I had to protect myself from being blindfolded and shot. That's why I carried a long, razor sharp knife. I used it three times."

They were out in the street now, and Jude was seeing still another side of Blackie's character. He had spoken so casually of cutting men's throats with a knife. Not many men in Texas cared to use such a weapon.

The two men went down to a café on the northwest corner of the square, ate breakfast, and Blackie ordered another fixed up to take over to Grady. He carried it out into the street. The town was quiet, only one saloon being open to catch the trade of the men who liked their morning drink. Dr. Vogel came by, on his way to get one.

"Morning," he grunted.

"Morning, Doc," Blackie replied. "How's Cic?"

"Demanding a drink of whiskey," snapped the other. "I was out of it—drank it all up last night and gave him the rest—and now I'm after a pint for him. It's not enough that I patch up their carcasses and remove bullets from their tough hides and get up in the middle of the night to fix broken noses and extract loose teeth knocked out in barroom fights. Almighty God, no! I've got to pack liquor for them to guzzle in *my* bed. Slept on the couch last night. Didn't sleep worth a damn either!"

He went toward the saloon, scowling, and Blackie laughed. "He's a rough and tough customer himself; as tough as any of the men he patches up. But he's a pretty nice old boy at that. Well, Jude, come on over with me while I give Grady his breakfast. He won't mind, and I want you to see the new jail anyhow. Sort of get you acquainted with it beforehand, in case you get into any more of these shooting scrapes."

"Are you keeping him here?" Jude asked as they crossed the street and entered the courthouse yard.

"All depends upon the Rangers. They're going to bring him over to the office in a little while and get a written confession out of him, which means that you'd better stay around. It happened in my jurisdiction, but because the murder of one of their men was involved they might take him out of here for trial, perhaps in Austin. You'd have to go up as a witness."

They went into the hallway and Blackie unlocked the door to his office. He came out with a large ring containing several big keys, one about six inches in length fitting the main door. They headed toward the new jail with its grim-looking bars in the windows, and Blackie unlocked the heavy door of sheet steel with riveted cross braces. He swung it wide.

There were three cells and Grady was in the far one. There

was no sound of movement, and Blackie called out, "All right, Grady. Roll out of that bunk. I've got your breakfast."

He paused and stared, they both stared, for Grady wasn't going to need any breakfast.

He hung by his belt from the side of the cell, his boots dangling three inches above the concrete floor.

"Good God!" Blackie burst out, and hurriedly set down the pail. He unlocked the door and they entered.

Jude followed him in and looked at the hanging rustler. Grady wasn't a very pretty sight. His head tilted over at a sharp right angle. His tongue was protruding, with little bubbles of dried froth around the corners of his mouth. The mouth was open, baring his buck teeth, and Grady seemed to be grinning at the wall, except for the protruding tongue. His hands hung lax at his sides.

"Get him around the legs, Jude, and lift him up," Blackie commanded, and stepped up into the blanketed bunk.

Jude took hold of the body, grasping it around the upper part of the legs. He lifted and Blackie leaned over and loosed the buckle of the belt enough to slip the improvised noose up over the dead brand blotter's head. The body came sagging down, but did not bend too far. *Rigor mortis* had set in.

Jude laid him in the bunk and stretched him out on his back. Some instinct caused him to bend the stiffened arms and make some kind of an effort to cross them over Grady's chest. A sleeve slid back and Jude saw that the skin around the wrist was chafed. Blackie's sharp eyes saw what was taking place. He looked at Jude.

"Seems to me he mighta changed his mind after looping that belt around his neck and tying the other end around to the top of the cell bars," he said. "I guess that when his wind got shut off he figured suicide wasn't such an easy out from a legal neck-breaking after all. I'd say he grabbed hard at the bars and fought to get back on the bunk, but didn't have the strength."

"It looks that way," Jude agreed.

But he noticed that one of Grady's feet was a little longer than the other. The boot was partly slipped off, cocked in place at the ankle. And Jude knew those marks on Grady's wrists were rope marks. His hands had been tied behind him before he was hung.

Saturday morning found a group of people on the porch of

110

Sol's store, watching the stage come in. It was loaded to over-flowing with very tired and bedraggled Easterners who had ridden all night. Jude, lounging against the wall of the store, waited. He smoked a cigarette, hat on the back of his head, right hip with the pistol thrust out, a thumb hooked in the cartridge belt. He heard a chorus of girlish greetings between Nell and two rather pretty girls about her age, watched Mrs. Travers introduce herself to two women and two well dressed businessmen.

They went off up the street to the hotel on the corner to allow the visitors a chance to clean up and eat breakfast. Jude had an idea that after they arrived back at the ranch the Stantons and Bordens would sleep most of the day until the evening festivities began. Bag after bag and trunk after trunk was unlashed and tossed down to be stacked on the porch.

Presently Bronson's stablehand, a youth named Toby, rattled up in a light livery rig. Jude helped him load all the baggage and watched him set off with it for the ranch. He debated having a morning drink, decided against it, and went up to kill time with Edwina in her shop until the others were ready to go. Blackie strolled by before Jude reached the shop.

"Going up to see Edwina?" he grinned.

"Thought I might," Jude said carelessly.

"You like her pretty well, don't you, Jude? Yeah," his tone a little edged, "and she likes you too. You wouldn't have any ideas about moving in on that range, would you, Jude?"

"If I get any, I'll try to move in, Blackie," was the quiet reply.

"Don't," the sheriff said coldly. "Don't ever make that foolish mistake, Jude. Edwina's still my woman and no man is going to cut in ahead of me, you or anybody else. You know," he went on in a milder tone, "it sorta looks like our trails have parted. There was a time when I figured that you and me could become pardners. But it seems at every turn of the road, Jude, I find you there either blocking it or compli-cating things for me. We're not the same kind of pardners we used to be. You were a green nester kid and I was the cowpuncher who got you started. Now you're a death-dealing gun fighter with six notches filed—"

"No notches, Blackie."

"—and I'm the lawman who's liable to either have to hang you or outlaw you. Looks like our trails not only have parted;

111

they've swung around until they're meeting head on. I hope I don't ever have to go after you, Jude."

"So do I."

"Well, I'll be moseying. And remember what I said: from now on you keep away from Edwina. She's my woman and I'll kill any man who tries to take her away from me."

So it was out in the open at last. Jude had known it was coming, felt the rising tide, the wide gulf that now separated them. They no longer were merely drifting on different trails.

They were enemies.

"Remember," Blackie warned, "don't go in that shop."

He moved off down the boardwalk toward Sol's store, the worn butts of the two heavy pistols bobbing to and fro with each step. Jude leaned there against the wall for a few moments. Then he too moved along the boardwalk. He went in and took off his hat.

"Hello, Jude!" Edwina greeted him. "I saw you come in. I was hoping you'd drop by."

CHAPTER TWENTY-FIVE

THE FESTIVITIES started Saturday just at sundown. All through the late afternoon rigs and riders on horseback had been arriving. The cut up parts of the butchered steer were still turning on the spits under Pokey's critical eyes. A big keg of whiskey had been set up not far from the veranda, with scores of tin cups on a table, and men and women were strolling over the grass, talking and laughing. And right beside the whiskey was a big box over which Nute Shelby kept a critical eye. It was filled with gunbelts and pistols. There was going to be no whiskey gunfight to mar the housewarming.

Long tables had been set up and on these Pokey laid cut up chunks of meat. It was warm and juicy, and there were pickles and heaping piles of biscuits and sweet bread to go with it.

Jude came up from the bunkhouse with his boots newly shined and his thick shock of finely spun hair slicked down.

He claimed Edwina for his first dance, floating across the smooth floor with her in a waltz. She danced as lightly as a feather, and beneath the silk handkerchief he held at the back of her waist to keep the sweat from soiling her dress, he felt the smooth play of her body.

She pushed back far enough to look at him. "Jude, I never dreamed you were such a smooth dancer. Where did you learn?"

"Up home among the nesters," he answered, and they both laughed.

He was unaware that over across the room Nell's eyes were expressing indignation. As the owner's daughter, she felt that he should have waited for her to have a dance free and then claim her. But the ranch punchers, putting down their first flush of bashfulness, had finally got started and were giving the three girls a busy time of it. Blackie was claiming dance after dance with Nell, whispering softly in her ear.

Edwina closed in close to Jude again. "Be careful, Jude," she whispered. "Blackie came into my room last night and warned me to keep away from you. He says that I'm still his woman and that I—that I'll be no other man's as long as he wants it that way. Jude, I'm getting a little afraid of him."

"I wouldn't let it worry you."

"I'm not worried about myself. He'll kill you."

"He might give it a try. I'll worry about that when the time comes."

He finally claimed Nell, who was properly indignant. They were quarrelling by the time the dance ended. There were a few more square dances and then the musicians put down their instruments and went out to refresh themselves at the barrel and to eat. It was along toward midnight. The two Rangers had come to the party, but had taken no part in the festivities except to have a couple of small drinks and chat amiably with the hands standing around the porch and watching through the doors and windows.

Then, as intermission set in, they went inside.

"Mr. Travers?" his wife said, in answer to a question by one of them. "Why, yes, Pa's in there in that other room. Right through that door there." She pointed.

"Thank you, ma'am," replied the younger.

They moved toward the door, the older man with the hard face trailing. They knocked and Travers' voice called, "Come in."

"Sorry to intrude, Mr. Travers," the younger man said. "We didn't know you had company."

"It's all right, boys. Mr. Stanton and Borden are talking

113

over some business with me. These men are Hardin and Renner, Texas Rangers working here to help stop this rustling."

Hardin shook hands and so did Renner. Hardin took the big roll of paper from beneath his arm.

"We could come back later," he suggested.

"Not at all. I presume it concerns the ranch, and these other men have a right to sit in and listen. They're going to invest out here and might as well start learning now."

Hardin unrolled the paper and spread it out on the table. It was criss-crossed with various lines that showed rivers and mountains and newly surveyed boundaries.

"Here's the set-up, Mr. Travers. Last year the Eight Cross outfit bought title to a big strip of land several miles long and three or four wide. That land goes over onto your boundary, or what you've always considered your boundary. It's legally owned by that ranch. We talked to Owsley, the foreman, up on the Cap Rock the other day, and he says he's about to start six hundred head grazing on that range. He also says you've got men up there with guns to stop him when he comes over."

"I have," Travers said harshly.

Hardin shook his head. "That's just the trouble. It's why we're here. The Texas Rangers are backing them up because they're in the right. They have title to that land, which will make you a trespasser. If you follow through what you say you aim to, we'll have to come after you with a warrant. If any Eight Cross man is killed, whichever one of your men does the shooting will hang or go to prison. We're down here to tell you to back up to the new boundary made by the surveyors."

It was a hard blow. It almost staggered Travers. He looked at the two silent Easterners and sighed. "You see what I was saying, men. I helped clear this country of the Comanches. My mother had her head split open by one of the red devils. I came back from the War, got my outfit together, and took over what I thought I was entitled to. Now they're buying land on my range, trimming me from all sides. They're using money from the sale of *my own* rustled cattle to whittle me down! A two-gunman named Red Tolliver, over to the south, slipped in and cut off two miles of my boundary along the river just the other day. And do you know what the cattle rustling son did? He registered a T iron with a mark that can be run over my 4 and make a perfect brand-blotting job—a kind of arrowhead. That's what he calls it. The TA. Gentlemen, I want to borrow enough money to buy up every foot of my present range. I want the deal swung as quickly as possible before they cut me down still more. Name your own terms and rate of interest, but get me that money!"

He turned to the two waiting Rangers. "All right, boys. I'll call off my men. That thieving outfit, burning my H Bar brand into an Eight Cross, is cleaning me. I know when I'm licked."

The Rangers thanked him and went out. There was silence in the room for a moment. The two Easterners exchanged glances. Finally Stanton spoke.

"All right, Travers. Get your surveyors to work at once and then let us know how much you need. You'll get it. A first mortgage on the ranch buildings and land and cattle, plus all equipment. I think you can come out all right."

CHAPTER TWENTY-SIX

IT WAS the summer of 1870. Abilene had had four years as a rip-roaring trail town. It had one more to go before, in 1871, new names would begin to spring up. Hays. Ellsworth. And the famed Dodge City, as the railroad pushed on farther west and swung south, making for shorter drives.

Jude worked the summer through on the ranch, riding from dawn until dark. He seldom went to town any more. Twice men fired at him from long range, and he sold the .44-40 repeater and bought himself a .42 caliber single-shot Sharps. It was heavy for a saddle gun, but it would throw a 550-grain slug of lead a lot farther than the powder charge back of the repeater's slugs. He grew shaggy-haired and silent, withdrawing more and more from bunkhouse life. There had been an election that summer and Blackie, with no opponent, was now duly elected Sheriff. Nobody else wanted the job in the face of what still could become a cattle war. Hardin and Renner had disappeared, gone like shadows. Travers owned his land now, barring the first mortgage held by the departed Easterners.

The outfit rolled in from Kansas again with only two punchers missing. One had quit. The other had been killed in a gun fight.

It had been a dry summer, the grass burned to a crisp. Nute Shelby hadn't gone up this year, sending another man as trail boss, a man who had been up twice before. Shelby rode all the hours of daylight, studying the lean cattle and looking at waterholes. He bought scrapers and put men to work down in the bottoms of the gullies and arroyos, peeling away at the red earth and using the dirt to make small dams.

The herd had brought a good price but not as much as the year before. Cattle by the tens of thousands were pouring up the trail, their owners eager to harvest the golden bonanza. Travers paid the slightly exorbitant rates on the mortgage, rode with Shelby, and shook his head. He was being rustled dry, some of his older stuff wouldn't come through the winter, and with so many of his stockers now already in the slaughterhouses his herds had fallen off alarmingly.

On the other hand, the Nester Pool herd had jumped to twenty-five hundred head. The Eight Cross was expanding. Red Tolliver swaggered about town, prosperous and contented. His TA iron was going on T4 cows and calves alike.

They made the fall roundup; and when it was over the results were appalling. Travers would be lucky if he could put two thousand head up the trail the next year.

Blackie and his two deputies had made some show of going after the rustlers. They had arrested four different men and presented what appeared to be solid evidence, but the jury had been packed with nester men who just as promptly freed them. However, the pool was breaking up now. It had become so prosperous that many of the men were now running small spreads of their own. They were living off the increases of the stock, buying more and rustling others. Their spreads were growing, a dozen new brands cropping up here and there.

It was the beginning of the heyday of the small cowman.

On a night that fall, when the weather began to turn a bit cold, the sheriff sat in the Eight Cross ranchhouse up on the Cap Rock. There were about thirty men present. These represented the north side of the pool. There were clouds of smoke from cigars, plenty of whiskey, and an air of well being. They had just finished dividing up the profits of the big drive to Abilene, most of it rustled from the T4 and quite a lot more from a couple of big spreads sixty miles north. The money had been counted out and put away when Blackie finally leaned back in his chair. He rose and flicked the ashes off a fifty-cent cigar. The buzz of voices gradually died down.

"Well, boys, it's been a good year and they'll get better. Now, shall I make a long speech or a short one?" he grinned.

Coarse laughter followed this. "Hell, we got plenty of time, sheriff. Tawk till you git outa breath."

"That means more or less to make it short. So I won't be too long. I called you up here for a little more than just to divide up the money each of you has coming according to the number of head he contributed to the pool's trail herd this year. I have, of course, already met with the boys down south and given them their share. I told them the same thing that I'm going to tell you. We're growing, but at the same time we've got to change our methods to meet changing conditions. The country's settling up that fast. In the beginning Travers and these other big owners far up north had up to forty or fifty square miles of range and sometimes more. They had cattle by the thousands and not too many men to handle them. It was a rustler's paradise—and, I might add, we made the most of it."

This one filled the room with a burst of coarse laughter.

"Now things are changing," Blackie went on in his smooth voice. "Your kids are growing up and going to their own schools and wearing decent clothes. They're eating something besides corn pone and molasses now. And it's up to you men to see to it that they grow up respectable. The kind of crude rustling that Grady got caught at is out. I want that clearly understood. Just about everyone of you now has enough cows to live off the increase and buy more with your profits. I want every man here to register his brand. Of course, if you get a chance to pick up a few calves here and there without risk, you can do it. If you can slip out in a bad rainstorm while the creek is flooded, it'll be all right to drive a few head down and shoot the cows and let them float downstream and take the calves. But any good thing has to come to an end, and the bonanza is over. The rustling we do from now on is going to be done by younger men picked for their jobs. Instead of stampeding a herd and running off two hundred head like we did that night up on Gramma Creek in Kansas, we'll have forty or fifty younger men of the pool pick out their calves, scout the lay of the land for days to check on the line riders, and play it safe.

"I can tell you now that Travers is hard hit. He bought his range all right, but he bought it with borrowed money from two Eastern financiers who're sinking their claws in for the interest on the loan. His T4 ranch is mortgaged to the hilt. I've been in touch with these two men—their names are Borden and Stanton—and I've painted a pretty black picture of Travers' position. I've got them worried. They're beginning to think they've made a bad investment. I told them that there was scab among Travers' cattle."

"But there ain't," a man's voice spoke up.

Blackie grinned at the speaker. "There will be," he said softly. "Red Tolliver has two hundred head of critters so covered with scab that they hardly have any hair left. I've never seen such mangy critters in all my life. As soon as the T4 brands that Red and some of the boys put on them heal a bit more they're going to be shoved over onto the T4 range and scattered among Travers' prime beef. We're going to put him out of business. And at the right moment, when Borden and Stanton, these two Eastern men, get bluffed enough to foreclose, I'm going to sell the T4 ranch at public auction on the courthouse steps in Alden, and that mortgage is going to be bought up by money from the Nester Pool!"

That one brought on a demonstration of sheer exuberance, partly whiskey and cigar-inspired. They slapped each other on the back, whooped and yelled. Only one man of them all beside Blackie stood silent: Jed Owsley. The cold-faced foreman of the Eight Cross stood with his hard back against the wall and said nothing. The noise finally quieted down. The men of the northern section of the pool resumed their seats.

Blackie looked them over. "Have I made everything clear?" he asked.

"Clear as we want it," a man's voice answered.

"All right. Then we're breaking up the Nester Pool as of tonight."

It got quiet in the room. They dropped their cigars low between fingers and stared at him. This they didn't understand.

"But you just said—" a man began.

"I said we'd buy up Travers' mortgage, bid in at public

118

auction when the time comes, with pool money. But each man will get range according to how much he contributes." Blackie's voice was sharp. "From now on it's up to each one of you individually. We'll go on rustling along the lines I just laid out. We've got to break Travers' back. From now on each of you who rustles a cow will do so at the risk of his own neck. The Rangers have drifted but the law has to be upheld. I'll arrest any man of you caught in the actual act of running off Travers' cattle. I want that clearly understood. Of course," he added with his goodnatured smile, "I'll try to pack the jury and see that you get off."

This one brought loud guffaws. Men looked at each other and grinned. Jed Owsley still stood with his back to the wall, a frown on his poker face.

"We'll work slow and carefully from now on," the sheriff continued. "We'll scab Travers' herd until they'll spend most of their time scratching instead of grazing. And one word of warning," he added sharply. "If you see a scabbed cow or calf up this way in the coming months, don't rustle it. Spot it! Make damned sure of that. When I sell Travers out at auction, and we buy up, we'll go out and clean the range, shooting and burning every carcass. Scab's a damned bad thing. That's about all I've got to say. Jed Owsley here is going to pick the younger men to do these special rustling jobs. The rest of you are going to rustle at your own risk. Any more questions?"

A man rose. He tossed the remains of his cigar to the floor.

"Yes, sheriff. You said we wuz to register all our brands. You own the Eight Cross. You goin' to register it? Any Ranger or anybody else could find out who owns it thet way. It mightn't look so good for you if people found out the Eight Cross is yore property."

"The ranch will be registered in Jed Owsley's name, as owner. We'll fix it up next week. Any more before I head back to Alden tonight?"

Owsley's shoulders moved away from the wall. He was as tall as Nute Shelby, nearly as blond.

"I've got one, Blackie. This sidewinder kid called Jude. First, you were going to bring him into the pool. Then you were going to take care of him so's he wouldn't cause us any more trouble. I hear he's still down on the T4."

"That's a fair question, Jed, and I'll answer it. I picked that kid up in Kansas because I figured he'd be a good man for

119

us. He proved it in Abilene when he killed Harrison, who was throwing a shot at my back. You all know—or don't you? —that I was supposed to kill Harrison. He had organized the pool. He was head of it. But he was so greedy that he was making each of you pay him a percentage of your cows on that fifteen hundred head the nesters sent north the first year. It was agreed that I was to take over in his boots, and he must have got wind of it somehow. I made two plays at him and he backed down before he finally tried to put one into me from behind while I was playing the roulette wheel. It was that nester kid Jude who grabbed one of my guns and did the job for me. He killed Harrison. I tried to swing him my way with a deputy's badge but it didn't seem to work. Before I hardly could turn around he'd got Tabor, Jergens, Porter, and those other two. But I warned him about several things, and you notice he's been pretty quiet these past months."

"Fair enough, Blackie," Owsley replied. "But he broke loose twice since he came back. Five men from the pool, plus Harrison. When's he going to do it again?"

"He won't, Jed. If he does I'll arrest him on sight and then bring in his body after he tries to 'escape.' Fair enough?"

The foreman grunted. "Fair enough, I reckon."

The meeting broke up and the sheriff started the long night ride back to Alden, feeling pleased with the world.

At the same moment Jude was in his bunk at the T4, wide awake and staring into the darkness while the others of the outfit snored soundly. He knew that conditions on the T4 were bad—far worse than Travers was admitting. He could see it in the drawn lines of Nute Shelby's face. But a puncher had to be loyal to his outfit, and thus Jude kept putting down the thoughts of saddling up one day and drifting.

The next day he got up and went back to work, and on a morning two weeks later he rode the south range. The line now had been pulled back more than three miles. Red Tolliver's cattle with that suspicious T brand followed by a crude arrowhead were on the old range farther south, along the river bluffs. Jude dropped down a gully, worked his horse up the opposite side, and then stopped to stare.

Then action followed look. He bent in the saddle, jerked the heavy Sharps free of its scabbard, and straightened. It went up to his shoulder and roared, and the cow a hundred yards distant went down under the shocking impact of the 550-grain slug of lead. Jude levered out the smoking shell, inserted another, and rode over. He pulled up and looked down.

It didn't have much hair. Where the hair had been was mostly a mass of scabs. It was the mangiest critter he had ever seen, and he knew that wherever it had brushed a mesquite or cedar limb along the trails it had left a trail of infection. He cut a wide circle and began to investigate. Within an hour he had shot four more. He went spurring down a gully after a fifth and the report of a rifle from two hundred yards away caused him to swerve sharply into the brush. He saw a faint cloud of smoke up on the ridge and heard the drumming of hoofs.

Jude slapped the steel to his bronk and went hard after the would-be drygulcher. He drove his mount mercilessly up in a scrambling climb to the top of a ridge and saw the rider.

Jude hit the ground as his horse slid to its haunches. He dropped to a knee, took careful aim with the .52 caliber single shot, and another cloud of gray smoke wisped up with the heavy report. The distant horse did a running somersault, throwing its rider overhead, and Jude went forward at a run on foot, reloading. He came up to the top of where a wood-rat's nest made a mound around the bole of a mesquite tree and saw his man. The other was down back of his dead horse, rifle up, peering.

Jude leveled the Sharps and aimed for the top side of the horse. He doubted that the slugs would pierce the carcass. He fired again and heard a startled yell, then broke down the side of the gully for a hundred-yard sprint in his high-heeled boots. When he came up again the man was still there. Slowly Jude lifted his hat dangling it on a stick. A spurt of dust leaped up beneath it and he let the headgear drop out of sight. The downed rider came up, rifle ready, cautious. Jud rose too, rifle cocked at his shoulder.

"Throw up your hands!" he yelled.

A rifle came up instead and Jude felt the heavy kick of the single shot against his own shoulder. He dropped flat, reloaded from the belt around his waist that was now half .44's and half .52's for the rifle, and then raised up once more. He got up and went forward, the gun halfway to his shoulder.

The rustler was down, his gun off to one side. Jude came closer to the horribly coughing man, substituting his six-shooter for the Sharps.

"How many of those scabs did you run over on our range?" he demanded.

"Go to hell," coughed out Red Tolliver.

"Anybody with you?"

"Go to hell."

"Who stampeded that herd up on Gramma Creek that night and shot Tolson? Who killed Jim Underhill? Who's the real head of this Nester Pool?"

"Blackie . . . all of 'em Blackie," Tolliver gasped out, a terrible grin contorting his mouth as the lashless lids opened wide. They they closed.

Red Tolliver was dead.

CHAPTER TWENTY-SEVEN

THREE RIDERS spurred into sight a short distance away, drumming hard, smashing down through the mesquite. They were bent over low in saddles.

"Don't shoot, Jude!" Mike Kessler yelled, straightening. "It's me—Mike!"

The two men with him were new men, line camp riders along the now whittled down south boundary. Jude lowered the Sharps and stood as they pounded up. They reined in hard.

"Holy cow!" Mike yelled again, swinging down. "Red Tolliver! You hurt, Jude?"

"No," Jude said. "I'm all right."

Then he told them everything: what had happened; what Red had gasped out as he lay dying; the set-up over which Blackie was overlord.

The two line riders sat their horses in silence, listening. The ever present buzzard sailed in the sky. A breeze whispered through the mesquite; and off in the distance a cow bellowed, the bawl of her calf coming in answer.

"So that's how it is?" Mike gasped out, amazement on his face. "He hung Grady to shut his mouth, eh?"

"That's right."

"And all the time I thought he used his belt on himself. What are you going to do now?"

"Going in to the ranch and make a full report to Nute and Travers. I'm going to tell them everything. So I'm burning the breeze. You boys scour this country and shoot every scab you see. If you don't this whole south range will be infected in a few months. You'll have to dip every head wearing a T4 brand. Hit out!"

He was unaware that he was giving orders and that they were obeying. Jude went back to where his horse stood with reins trailing and caught it. He swung up and made the seven miles back to the ranch in good time.

He went directly to the horse corral and unsaddled. He saw no movement of life around the ranch. A rooster crowed in the chicken pens. A milk pen calf bawled. Smoke wisped up lazily from the dugout dining room. The late morning sun shone down; there was no breeze in the air.

The cream-colored sorrel was in the corral, fresh and rested. Jude went in with his rope, saddled the sorrel and threw his reins up over the animal's neck. He swung aboard the short, blocky body and rode up to the house.

Mrs. Travers was on the porch above the kitchen, peeling a batch of potatoes and chatting with Jessie, who sat beside her.

Jude reined up, but didn't get down.

"Seen Nute or the boss around?" he asked.

"They rode off about eight this morning, Jude. They're down on the south range somewhere."

"Where's Miss Travers?"

"So you finally are getting interested in our daughter, are you, Jude? I'm glad. Nell's in town. She left about sunup. I think they're giving some kind of a reception for some woman who's going to have a baby. You know, gifts and all that."

"All right," Jude said.

He reined over and rode down across the flats.

He let the blocky cream sorrel take its time and didn't get into town until after two o'clock that afternoon. He rode first to Edwina's shop, but the woman who now was helping her said that she was out taking one of the afternoon rides in which she sometimes indulged. Nell Travers was with her.

Jude left the sorrel in front of the dress shop and walked down the street. He saw two men, tensed, and then relaxed as he recognized the two Texas Rangers, Hardin and Renner. They came up and shook hands. A man, one of the nesters, leaned against a wall nearby. He eyed the trio with brittle eyes.

"Hello, puncher," Hardin greeted Jude quietly. "How's things been going?"

"All right, I guess. Seen Blackie around?"

They looked at him sharply. "You seem kind of nervous, son," Renner said. "Blackie's out of town. Oughta be back most any time now. We sorta wanted to talk to him, too. Anything special you wanted to see him about?"

Quietly Jude told them everything. He did it aware that the man leaning against the wall had sidled off down the street toward where his horse was racked, that Sol Martin stood in the doorway of his big store, listening.

"So thet's how it is," Hardin said softly, and pulled thoughtfully at his chin.

"That's how it is," Jude said.

"Going to submit to arrest on charges of killing this Red Tolliver?"

"No. It was justified. He was driving scabbed cattle over onto our range, and he fired the first shot. You can probably find the empty shell. I came in to call Blackie's hand. He warned me and I know what to expect."

"So it's going to be a shoot-out?" Hardin asked. "He's a lawman, you know. That means the Rangers will have to act."

"I know," Jude answered.

Hardin let a grim smile come over his usually taciturn face. He reached up into a short pocket and extracted a white paper. Renner spoke up.

"Son, we've had our eye on you for a long time now. You've got the makings of a good Texas Ranger. Hardin here is a captain in the service. He wrote a recommendation to Austin for you to come in with us. There's your commission and your badge."

Hardin had held out the paper in one hand. In the other was a metal badge. "They're yours, Gordon," he said, smiling. "We want you in the service."

Jude looked at them. Slowly he shook his head.

"There's two women involved. One of them was Blackie's girl, and he gave me orders to keep away from her. The other is one he's been trying to marry. Then there was Tolson, the puncher who was shot that night he stampeded the trail herd. He had Tolson murdered. One of the nesters did it, just who I don't know and probably will never learn. But I was one of the outfit, and I still am."

"Loyalty," Hardin said, returning badge and paper to his short pocket. "The blind loyalty that cowpunchers have for their outfits. That and women. I wish I knew how many men have been shot, imprisoned, and hanged for it. So it's going to be a shoot-out? You know what that means, of course?"

"Yes, I know," Jude nodded. "But it's got to be that way."

"He's fast, son," Renner said. "He might get you."

Hardin sighed. He glanced at the rack where their horses stood with rifles in the scabbards.

"Maybe we can get around it," he said to the older man. "Let's go over to Blackie's office and wait for him."

Jude stood watching them as they crossed to the new red courthouse and disappeared through the tunnel-like entrance of the hallway running north and south. He was aware that Sol was frozen in the doorway of his store, his son beside him; that a murmur had gone up and down the street. It was about then that Blackie and the man who had been leaning against the wall reentered town, riding past the old and now deserted sheriff's office. The other had caught him just a short distance out of town and told him everything he had overheard. Blackie knew. He was facing it. Jude saw the careless swing of his hands as he reined up and dropped to the ground in a single, lithe step. The other man hurriedly rode across to the north side of the square where men were watching.

Blackie came along the west side of the square, his boots making hard sounds on the dried boardwalk. He was as handsome as he had been that first day when he had come out of a barber's chair in Abilene and gone back to the gun shop with Jude to pick out the pistol that now lay in the sheath at Jude's right thigh.

Jude shook the gun in its sheath to loosen it and started moving toward him. He came to where Sol Martin stood in the doorway of his store, and suddenly Sol stepped out and threw his fat arms around him.

"No, no, boy!" he cried out. "No, no, Jude! Don't meet him. He'll kill you. Give me that gun, Jude, and I'll back you up with everything I've got. Don't do it, boy!"

Over in the courthouse office of the sheriff the two Rangers stood looking through the west window.

"The kid's going down," Captain Hardin said. "He hasn't got a chance. But he wanted it that way. By God, what a Texas Ranger he would have made! Anyhow, it'll clinch this warrant I have for Blackie being owner of the Eight Cross. He thought the Rangers had slid out and were asleep after Durton got killed. He thought I didn't see those rope marks on that rustler's wrists when we held the inquest. And now they're coming down the walk toward each other. That kid's just flung Sol Martin's hand off him and is moving on. If Blackie kills him we'll still have to serve this warrant. And if the kid should come out on top, we've got to run him down and bring him in for downing a lawman. Look—!"

"My money's on the kid," Renner whispered hoarsely.

Over on the boardwalk, they had come to a stop some thirty feet distant. Blackie paused, and the old smile came to his handsome face.

"Hello, pardner," he greeted Jude. "I've been hearing things."

"They get around, I reckon," Jude said.

"So you got Red?"

"He talked a little before he died. I think I know now who rattled that slicker that night up in Kansas and shot Tolson. I think I got a gretty good idea of why you were so set on killing Harrison in Abilene—because you wanted to take over as head of the Nester Pool. I know who hung Grady that night in his cell, hitting him over the head with a gun to stun him before lashing his wrists and swinging him by his belt, and then pulling down on his boots to strangle him. I could have overlooked some of that, Blackie, but you told me to keep away from Edwina and you're trying to marry a girl like Nell. That's what I couldn't take."

"So you're in love with one of them?" sneered Blackie.

"Yes," Jude said. "I'm in love with one of them."

The window of Blackie's office was now up and the two Rangers peering through, listening. A half-dozen horses at hitchracks switched flies with their tails, dozing lazily. The air was clear, clean. It was split by the crash of six-shooters. Smoke from black powder roiled up around Jude's stomach as he thumbed shot after shot, for Blackie was down and still trying to fire. Jude took deliberate aim and killed him with a final shot.

He turned. His left arm had a hot branding iron running across it above the elbow, while a stream of blood flowed down the skin and dripped from his wrist. He saw the cream sorrel up there a hundred yards away and he broke into a run. He went past Sol's store, shoving the gun back into its sheath, leaving a man down on the boardwalk. A man who wore a lawman's badge.

Jude took his saddle in a bound, grabbing up the reins with his good arm. The face of a frightened woman looked out from Edwina's store. Some strange instinct caused her to cry out, "She an' Miss Nell ain't here. They went riding!" He ignored her because there was no time. A few minutes before he could have been a lawman. In a few short minutes since then, he had become a desperado, a man wanted by the law for killing a lawman. He had to get out fast, leaving behind the woman he so desperately loved, the woman he had loved all those long lonesome months.

He roweled the now rested cream sorrel, biting at his bandana with his teeth and knotting it around his useless left arm. He swung westward, toward the open prairie, and the town and all that it had become to him fell behind. The sorrel's blocky body rocked beneath him as he finished cutting off the blood flow and looked back. He let the animal take its time; that much he had learned about working a cow horse. Now he saw the two riders far behind, the Rangers who were after him, and he saw the two riders ahead too.

He came abreast of them, his left arm afire, bandaged, bloody. He pulled up.

"Jude, what's happened!" Edwina cried out.

He told her and Nell in terse sentences that took seconds. The two pursuing riders were coming hard.

"You killed Blackie?" Nell screamed. "You couldn't have! We were to have been married. . . ."

He didn't hear the rest of it. He was looking at Edwina, at her golden hair and her lovely face.

"Jude, they're coming! *Go, go!*" she cried to him.

"I'm heading for Santa Fe, Mexico territory, first stop, then on into Arizona territory," he said, and rode closer. "I guess I've always loved you, Edwina. It looks like good-bye."

"Jude, you can't! I love you, too! But I was Blackie's girl. I'm . . ."

"Meet me there. I'll wait for you."

"Jude, go, go, go! They're coming!"

127

"I'm waiting for an answer."

"You have it. Wait for me, darling. Oh, Jude, wait for me in Santa Fe! Now run for it!"

He ran for it. Hardin and Renner were roweling hard across the flats. They went past the two women with long reins slashing down across the flanks of their fresh horses, burning the wind after the rider astride the cream sorrel with four white feet. They came to a rise and Hardin held up a hand.

"My horse seems to have got a limp," he grunted. "We never coulda caught him."

Renner said, "So's mine. He always was a shortwinded cuss anyhow." And his eyes went to the shirt front of his superior. Captain Hardin had taken a paper from his shirt pocket and was tearing it to bits. He took out the badge and looked at Renner, who reached a hand for it.

Renner said, "I'll betcha I can hit that prairie dog's hole with this," and tossed.

It was a good shot. The badge went rumbling into the bowels of the earth. Renner sat his horse, looking at the distant rider.

"You damned old outlaw," Hardin chuckled. "I'll bet that right this minute your heart's right out there with that desperado kid. I oughta shoot you."

Renner grinned back at him, his hard face softening. "He sure saved us a lot of trouble a second time, Jim. And I reckon the Texas Rangers allus oughta pay their debts."

Ahead of them Jude was still working the cream sorrel, throwing quick glances over his shoulder. He had confidence in the horse that once had thrown him so hard.

He turned in the saddle and the breeze struck his face, pushing his hat brim up, and filling his soul with a strange kind of new happiness.

He bent forward and the cream sorrel leveled its neck out, carrying him lunging into the West . . . toward Santa Fe and a rendezvous with a lovely, golden-haired woman.

The End